Praise for
tor'cha

"Todd Craig's writing can hold more weight than the mighty 59th St. Bridge during rush hour. He is a combo of Zora Neale Hurston and Bonz Malone. A classic New York slice of pizza, hold the swine…"

Bobbito Garcia
DJ and Author *Where'd You Get Those? New York City's Sneaker Culture: 1960-1987* (Testify Books)

"Todd Craig's *tor'cha* is a book that compels his readers to think of scriptural commands with hip hop flavor and Supreme Mathematics as it's applied to one's life in relationship to the grand scheme of the universe. *tor'cha* will get'cha to think about Supreme Mathematics and Knowledge add a Cipher—the Ten Commandments—that brought'cha into existence to righteously rule the universe!"

Allah B
The renowned Elder of the Nation of Gods & Earths
Executive Director of Allah School in Mecca

"From the Ten Commandments through Supreme Mathematics, Todd Craig weaves a head spinning tale that captures New York—its intoxicating highs as well as its gritty lows—with an unblinking eye."

HS Miller
Writer and Director of "Anamorph" (IFC / Kamala Films)

"Todd Craig takes readers deep into the darkness in order to show us the light. Written in a street-smart style, this book should be required reading for anyone taken in by the glamorization of the gangsta culture."

Geoffrey Canada
President and CEO, Harlem Children's Zone

"*tor'cha* is a remarkable book, a credit to the writer and to the adventurousness of Swank Books. To contain such powerful themes and feelings within a controlled work is a special credit to the writer. Virtually every minute reading the book I feel I am walking through a field of potential land mines—hyperbole, rant, black despair, naked unrestrained polemics, etc. What I get instead is passion and at the heart of that passion faith, hope, and love—just what the good book says. Not to say that there isn't hideous suffering and tragedy, but it seems to me never irredeemable."

Eugene Garber
Author of *Vienna øø*

"Todd Craig is a brilliant young writer. His first book, *tor'cha*, is the riveting account of the spiritual odyssey of urban youth. The powerful journey draws the reader into complex relationships of love, hate and compromise. In the process of shaping his characters, Craig raises pivotal questions concerning the silent war that rages in inner cities across the nation. Read this book and ponder the answers that can lead us to hope."

Dr. Bessie W. Blake,
Author of *Speak to the Mountain*
(USA Book News '07 Best Book Award)

"Todd Craig's *tor'cha* shines the light on the duality of neighborhood life for our youth: the street philosophy and codes and its antithesis—religion. Backed by music that takes you deeper into the fold by creating an atmosphere of pain, anger, and shock, this is not just a read but an experience."

Mr.LeN
"Lunchtime with Mr. Len"
www.xxlmag.com

"The challenge with Black literature is to keep it relevant to the target audience while also securing a place in the larger body of world literature. The problem with a large part of what 'passes' as Black literature is that it is just fast-food black (yeah a small 'b') literature. It is only reflective of a small segment of Black life. It also offers nothing to that segment. It doesn't get to the root of issues, it doesn't connect it to larger problems, and it doesn't offer solutions. *tor'cha* is that answer. It has layers that allow you to dig deeper and deeper into it. It connects with that street youth on the corner while at the same time can be found in the backpack of a college student at a historically Black college. Each layer is a meal. The same way that people like Hype Williams and Spike Lee innovated cinematic techniques with video and movies can be manifested in writing. Todd Craig has a magnetic story style that is all his own and will draw you in."

C'BS Alife,
Original Thought Magazine
www.originalthoughtmag.com

"The symbiotic relationship between the book and CD opens the reader up to an entirely new experience in fiction. This brilliant stories-with-soundtrack format creates a similar experience to that of watching a movie, except that this experience allows the reader to provide their own visual content, driven by the printed text, the soundtrack, and the combination of both. By breaking down everyday situations into lowest common spiritual denominators based on the overlap between Biblical Scriptures and Supreme Mathematics, Craig springs forth as a sort of urban prophet illuminating the underbelly of Queens as a microcosm for global society. Craig's uncompromising verbal technique takes readers on a visceral roller coaster ride through the bosom and bowels of the Projects, only to emerge from the dark tunnel awestruck, like a pair of eyes encountering the blinding clarity of daylight after a ride on the subway."

Dinorah de Jesús Rodriguez
South Florida Times
http://alternativeage.blogspot.com

"To grow up in Hip-Hop means more than just listening to the music or throwing up some aimless tag on a subway car. It means growing up in an environment where people are often filled with the same kind of abysmal introspection Ghostface Killah is imbued with on *Can It All Be So Simple*. Luckily, there are writers within the genre who keep with James Baldwin's assertion that 'all art is a kind of confession' in which all artists have an obligation to themselves and their craft to 'vomit' up the truth. Todd Craig is one such writer."

Malcolm Nelson
Liberator Magazine
www.liberatormagazine.com

...tor'cha...

(tor • ture)

A novel by
Todd Craig

Swank Books • Boston

2nd printing, January 2009

Cover art and design by Che Tucker Barron, Jeremy Portje &
Israel Rosas
Dedication photo by HS Miller
Author photo by Rachel Crick

Printed in the United States

LIBRARY OF CONGRESS
CATALOGING-IN-PUBLICATION DATA
Todd Craig, 1974
    tor'cha / Todd Craig – 2nd American ed.
    ISBN: 978-0-9744288-4-0

Swank Books
P.O. Box 300163
Jamaica Plain, MA 02130

www.swankbooks.com

blacker inkwells publishing
www.blackerinkwells.com

Ten Commandments, brothers branded
Higher than life occurrences in the hood
Landed
On top of the shoulders of soldiers
Lost in the armor created by physical karma

So many battles
Drugs, Guns, Death, equal Life
In a hood filled with strife

Can you **feel** the pain?
Are there words that drain?
Harder than what commandments have told
Maybe if the guns uncock in the hood
Then our brothers can stand up bold!

Face the tablets as the words echo in your inner ear
Before you break that word, listen clear
Thou shall not kill!
So instead you steal?
Avoiding every other commandment against His will

Will he or she listen to He?
To preserve a better community for we
Or does denial come in full revival
Emptying out the future of our survival
There is too much doubt

Walking the line is divine
Step off, back on now
In time
The line will strengthen the balance in your mind

For if your mind strays the body shall follow
Then your spirit echoes as the voices reveal the hollow
Inside the mind of your thinking
Sober moments give way as if you're constantly drinking
So stay in the grind of the lines the commandments have taught'cha

Or forever live in eternal tor'cha

Takbir Blake
Peace by Piece

...I had my man say a prayer for me so I could go in...

Foreword

The first thing that happened when I opened this book was a realization of the sacredness of the voyage that Todd Craig had set out for me. I started with *Peace by Piece* and used that, almost like a dictionary—but more than that, to understand what *tor'cha* is... And then I entered into the power of the Ten Commandments and Supreme Mathematics in the Preface. Here, you will understand real quick why I am calling this novel a kind of sacred encounter. For those of you unfamiliar with these eternal doctrines, trust in the power that their words evoke... and let that trust guide your reading.

The way I see it, there are three tasks in front of you, three ways to go in and come back out of this book, otherwise you will be lost, and miss out on the world that Todd Craig is giving us.

Task One... People Get Ready

If what you are used to or looking for is the kind of novel that sometimes gets called "urban fiction" where you experience a kind of voyeurism into the destruction of black folks lives and humanity, this book will be a new experience for you. This is not one of them *ShaVenereal and Her New Pimp Kill They First Trick and Steal a New Benz* kind of things. And don't even front, you know the kind of books that I mean, you might even like some of them (you may as well cop to it). It's not that those stories are not important, real, or humanly possible, it's just that those books mostly give you the ghetto-fabulous-er version of a Jerry Springer episode that can never do justice to the realities that get exploited. Now don't get it twisted, *tor'cha* IS a book about the hood, from the "hardrocks and hustlas to the stick-up kids and conflicted crackheads", but these are not social mutants and misfits featured in a circus freakshow. These are the "characters who all had supporting roles in this motion picture called life," in all of our lives, whether you live near or far from them. The fantas-gasmic hood fiction only tells you half of a story that ain't never been told about these characters — what we need instead is what Todd Craig gives us: characters at their early and final demise, lashing out on one another and their own selves, in full frenzy and anger and pain and bitterness and human rage that is so real and yet verbally intangible. But, also, here in this book, in this most sacred Mathematics and Commands of Life, we see things all the way through: the places where people's minds and soul and bodies have really been beforehand; and then all the stank, grime, hard-to-sweep-away ashes that are left after the fire is gone when the world burns them up. This book will give you the fire below and above, before and after, here and now. So, make sure, before you go in, that you have really asked yourself: am I ready for that?

Are you ready for a love so strong that it contradicts the world that doesn't love all of its human beings equally? Can you walk with Ayesha into that world and decide, with her, if you can stay or if you must go? Are you ready for Chris/Christian, Re-Christened and Re-Christed, "disciplined in the archery of academia... with a creative energy that emanated from a place he had been destined to rep for a long time"?

Are you ready for eM/Emil who "slice[s] the waves of sound so that [your] eardrum would vibrate until [your] heart felt what he was feeling", even when his heart carries too much for him to bear?

Are you ready for the supra-world bond between Chris and eM, brothers/cousins/twinned souls in different places but in the same mental space?

Are you ready for Damon, Deem, his Demons, and "his rebirth, as Abdullah Zahir, walking hand in hand with Allah" as his mental-spiritual docs battle with his physical?

Are you ready for "ghetto alchemists" who pull "white sheetrock from out the salt mines and into the poisoned populous" who control so many but don't always see what's coming from the populous?

Are you ready for Jerry—the elegant and wise can't-be-taken-down mentor/father/teacher whose role and role-modeling get redesigned?

You know these people, you feel these people, you see them in your own window or even in your own mirror everyday so can you let Todd Craig give em to you in a new way now?

Task Two… "writerightritewrightwrite"
Now, for those of you who are or aspire-to-be the literati, or even the Niggerati, as Zora Neale Hurston put it back in the day, and have (or will) authorize yourself to talk about this *tor'cha*. You might have even more "readying" to do if you stay stuck on stupid by concocting bourgeois-

only vocabulary and rules about-how-to-dissect-literature to talk about a world that ain't bougsie, to talk in ways that won't ever relate to, understand, compliment, demand, or re-create the world that the people in *tor'cha* live. For the youngheads out there, the HipHopHeads, the ones still reppin' they block no matter what, the ones rejecting stereotypes of the hood as pure pathology, the ones not marketing the hood for white-rebellious-fantasies-of-bein'-down, the ones still street-conscious even when you ain't in the streets: beware, don't let the literati get you caught up. If you know what it was like to be hungry, to not have the lights turned on, to stand on line to ask for food, or to see someone you love behind bars or in a casket, you know how real this book is. For those of you lucky to be born somewhere, sometime else where you did not have to know this kind of reality, but you still want to fight the world that would ignore these pillars of social reality, then you know this book is real too. When you talk about *tor'cha*, do it in new terms, real terms, in *your terms* and make sure that the literati around you do the same. This is not the story of the Bourgeoisie or the Super-Negroes/Minority-Extraordinaires who follow the rules so they can get up and leave. This is about that place that eM goes to when he writes, "curled at the back sitting on the bed, elbows resting upon his knees...in that position...for hours on end, and rock[in] to the same beat." Remember that place, why eM needs that place for his sanity and mental survival, read as if you were right there with eM, and then make sure that the discussion of this *tor'cha* matches where eM goes, has to go.

Task Three... *Itchin for a Scratch*

As you leave this world/book, know that *tor'cha* is giving you new ways to think about who a writer is and can be; how writing can look, what it can sound like, and even what the soundtrack would be, for both the process along the way and the final product at the end. Some of you might even got a little of the itch to write yourself, might even be full scratchin. You just go right on 'head and do it.... *Til ya satissssfiiiiiiied*. I say that with all my heart and with every part of my being right now because if you are in schools/gov'ment institutions, almost no one who is supposedly "official" will tell you how official Todd Craig's book right here is for you—its style, its lessons, its rhythms, its grammars, its vernaculars, its memories—it is who and what you can be every single time that you write to shape knowledge of your self in this world. Yes, each and every time. Think back on all them new dialects "through rhyme and reason" that Todd Craig told you about. Just cuz no one tells you that you can be that, that you can be something different, just cuz they deny that to/for you, don't you forget your human possibility. Let the words that you write be the thoughts that you are, let it be like the music that plays throughout this novel—"a way of life... out of life's confines" and into freedom.

I wish you well on your path to fulfilling these three tasks... I'll see you on the other side...

Carmen Kynard, Ph.D.
St. John's University, Queens, NY
Department of English
January 2009

Preface

For a richer experience reading this novel, some understanding of its theological and spiritual currents is necessary. The first component involves understanding the Ten Commandments, as each of the chapters is based on the idea of a character either about to, in the midst of, or having already broken one of the Commandments.

As the story is told in Exodus, after God told Moses to lead the Israelites out of Egypt and across the Red Sea, God called him to the top of Mount Sinai and gave him the Ten Commandments, instructing him to write them on two stone tablets.

The first three Commandments were inscribed on the first tablet:

1 I am the Lord thy God, which have brought thee out of the land of Egypt, out of the house of bondage. Thou shalt have no other gods before me.

2 Thou shalt not make unto thee any graven image, or any likeness of any thing that is in heaven above, or that is in the earth beneath, or that is in the water under the earth: thou shalt not bow down thyself to them, nor serve them: for I the Lord thy God am a jealous God, visiting the iniquity of the fathers upon the children unto the third and fourth generation of them that hate me; and shewing mercy unto thousands of them that love me, and keep my commandments.

3 Thou shalt not take the name of the Lord thy God in vain; for the Lord will not hold him guiltless that taketh his name in vain.

The remaining seven Commandments were written on the second stone as:

4   Remember the sabbath day, to keep it holy. Six days shalt thou labour, and do all thy work: but the seventh day is the sabbath of the Lord thy God: in it, thou shalt not do any work, thou, nor thy son, nor thy daughter, thy manservant, nor thy maidservant, nor thy cattle, nor thy stranger that is within thy gates: for in six days the Lord made heaven and earth, the sea, and all that in them is, and rested the seventh day: wherefore the Lord blessed the sabbath day, and hallowed it.

5   Honour thy father and thy mother: that thy days may be long upon the land which the Lord thy God giveth thee.

6   Thou shalt not kill.

7   Thou shalt not commit adultery.

8   Thou shalt not steal.

9   Thou shalt not bear false witness against thy neighbour.

10 Thou shalt not covet thy neighbour's house, thou shalt not covet thy neighbour's wife, nor his manservant, nor his maidservant, nor his ox, nor his ass, nor any thing that is thy neighbour's.

The Holy Bible, King James Version,
Exodus 20 : 2-17

The first three Commandments were instructions on how Christians were to engage with God. This is indeed a "mysterious" relationship; Christians believe in the notion of God as a Being or an unseen Spiritual force. The critical question becomes how does a person engage in a relationship with a Being absent in physical form, and present only in spiritual essence? One must simply have blind faith that God is there, always seeing and omnipresent.

The remaining seven Commandments were based on people's relationships with one another. Jesus later summarized the idea behind this group of Commandments with The Golden Rule: Do unto others as you would have them do unto you. Depending on how devout or spiritual an individual may be, his or her conversations with God may be ongoing or few and far between. The variable relationship with God versus that of humanity within the Commandments informs the journey described in this book.

The second component of this novel is the moral of each story, captured by the notion of Supreme Mathematics in Islam. To explain this idea properly, I met with George Khaldun and Allah B. Mr. George Khaldun is the Chief Operating Officer of the Harlem Children's Zone. Originally entering the Muslim community as a member of the Nation of Islam forty-four years ago, he has emerged with a deeper understanding of the teachings of the Honorable Elijah Muhammed and the Koran; he now respects and embraces all schools of thought within Islamic culture that engage Allah as the one true and living God. Allah B is esteemed as one of the "first fruits" and primary students of the Nation of Gods and Earths. Allah B is an elder in the Nation and influential in bringing the knowledge to the Bronx, New York.

In his second trip, Islamic scholar WD Fard brought Supreme Wisdom from the Holy City of Mecca to the shores of North America in the early 1900's. Through his teachings of Islam, the aspect of Supreme Wisdom was taught in the impoverished Paradise Valley section of Detroit, also known as Detroit's "Black Bottom." In 1931, WD Fard met and taught the Wisdom to Elijah Poole, who was later known as The Honorable Elijah Muhammed— leader of the Nation of Islam. Having studied in his country for 20 years, WD Fard came with the Wisdom and approached it differently from anything else manifested as scriptures. Supreme Wisdom was a way of life that entailed a person first acquiring wisdom. This wisdom leads a person to be "divine" and thus the pursuit of knowledge begins. The daily experience of an individual putting wisdom and knowledge into practice brought about understanding—the culminating point of this process. The key to Supreme Wisdom is putting it to use in order to change one's life: Khaldun explained that "Supreme Wisdom is based on the keys to change your life and make you supreme, but you have to put it to work. Otherwise, it remains 'dead letter'—it's just a word, but it means nothing, it's useless if not put to practice." The Honorable Elijah Muhammed began to teach this Wisdom from a religious perspective within Islamic rituals. Regis-tered Muslims couldn't rise through the ranks of Islam with-out an understanding of this Wisdom. One of The Honorable Elijah Muhammed's most prolific students was Clarence13X.

After returning from the Korean War, Clarence 13X went through this registration process in 1960. Over the course of two to three years, he quickly rose through the ranks and became a Lieutenant in the Fruit of Islam (F.O.I.): the military branch of the Nation of Islam. A Korean War veteran and karate expert, he taught and trained the F.O.I. In describing Clarence 13X, Allah B said "He was questioning things the people should've questioned but didn't—he took nothing at face value." One of his most important philosophical questions was "if the original man is a black man, then must man be God?" In other words, if the original man is a black man, and man is made in God's image, then must the black man be God? Clarence 13X began to question the practical application of Supreme Wisdom, leading him to a different interpretation. While there are a number of varying and contrasting accounts, Clarence 13X inevitably separated from the Nation of Islam.

Upon leaving the Nation of Islam, Clarence 13X changed his name to Allah, The Father and took his understanding of Supreme Wisdom directly to the streets, founding the Five Percent Nation of Islam. He began to apply the Wisdom differently—switching the order of the principles from "wisdom, knowledge" to "knowledge, wisdom." With this change Allah, The Father conceived Supreme Mathematics: a set of universal principles governing experience, know-ledge and belief. These 10 numbers were designated as:

1-knowledge
2-wisdom
3-understanding
4-culture
5-power
6-equality
7-God (Allah)
8-build/destroy
9-born
0-cypher

In his teachings, Allah, The Father wanted to make sure he was a brother to his followers as opposed to a figurehead, and this allowed him to spread the knowledge amongst the youth in Harlem. Allah, The Father saw knowledge first as the foundation of all things. He found that WD Fard and Elijah Muhammed's understanding was not wrong, but simply limited. Allah, The Father did not want to be restrictive in this way but instead teach and spread the "knowledge of self" to the streets, engaging the street-corner society with the knowledge. This designated the separation between the Nation of Islam and the Five Percent Nation of Islam. After Allah, The Father's assassination in 1969, Five Percenters began to refer to themselves as "The Nation of Gods and Earths." People began to relate to the Nation of Gods and Earths because they were put at ease by their everyday appearance in dress and speech; they looked like everyday people. What differed was these street-smart individuals would speak and demonstrate having "knowledge of self."

Allah, The Father articulated the knowledge in a way that opened a new world for youth so they could understand it not only literally, but also from social, political and philosophical perspectives. It was through this knowledge that a large number of disenfranchised youth – many of whom were either in junior high school or high school dropouts – began to understand the concept of the "haves" and "have nots" not simply from a local, but also a global vantage point. After Supreme Mathematics, Allah, The Father brought forth the Supreme Alphabet, and similar to the Nation of Islam's registration, the process for followers to learn this information was to write it down, memorize it and destroy the paper.

Supreme Mathematics differed from spiritual information given to religious followers from priests, imams and pastors, because the math was given directly to the people, and allowed them to apply it to their world and surroundings. It empowered people of varying race and class, who were not only powerless, but also disenfran-chised. Supreme Mathematics involved finding in num-bers living characters keyed to the operations of the universe and described in the language of science. It was part of the spiritual teachings that could be used as guidelines to living justly, in theory, a key to the universe that would unlock the answers to all the questions in life. This is the second fundamental concept that drives the stories in this novel.

A Lesson in Supreme Mathematics

Supreme Mathematics

1-knowledge
2-wisdom
3-understanding
4-culture
5-power
6-equality
7-God (Allah)
8-build or destroy
9-born
0-cypher

Lesson in addition: Each letter of the alphabet bears a numeric value. Once these values are added, you continue to add the numbers until you reach a number between 1-9. The final sum is what is "born."

For example:

Question: What does the author's name "born"?

As readers, we know the author's name is Todd—with that we proceed as follows:

Step One: Find each letter's numeric value:

T - 20
o -15
d - 4
d - 4

Step Two: Add each value together:

20 + 15 + 4 + 4 = 43

Step Three: Continue to add each number until it has become a number between 1-9:

43 = 4 + 3 = 7

Step Four: Once a value between numbers 1-9 has been found, refer to the list of Supreme Mathematics to find its philosophical value:

Answer: 7 = God

Thus, the author's name Todd "borns" God

In this particular case, the word "born" will be a synonym for the word "equal." In reading, this is a critical piece for understanding why so many things are "born."

One can now proceed with the reading, after this brief lesson on Supreme Mathematics.

Dedication

To Uncle Dea Mill, Aunt Skinny, Killer Black...

...and also

"...to the hood..."

...I have been captured and taken to the enemy's prison...and because I will not talk, the general commands his troops to prepare the prelude for the actions to be committed against me entitled...

Six years ago when I sat down to write this, I was in a very strange place. I was almost halfway through, struggling to breach past that point. Really, it was my worse enemy tryin' to put a bug in my ear, telling me I couldn't do it, couldn't finish. Now I know that enemy was me. And I was so consumed with what some people around me were saying, with the entire notion of fact versus fiction, whether it was real or just a novel. It's tough to write a prologue from that place. But now, I see the picture differently. There's not a question as to whether it'll get finished or not, because it's here now. So being able to rock with hindsight as twenty-twenty, I figured it was a real good time to check in with y'all and really let you know what you're about to get yourself into...

The one thing I've said in this process as it comes to a close is I really need to think about what I title books now, because I never want a title coming back to bite me in the ass. For truly, this has been torture on a whole lotta levels. For one, I've taken on quite a task here, and I don't know if anyone else would have the heart to do it. I got a lot goin' on here, and really, what I'm trying to do is bridge a lot of gaps. See, the way I look at it, we have been led to believe

1

anything that has to do with Islam is deviant to a certain extent. For real...it becomes more about blowing up buildings and anonymous lost videotapes found months later that depict our understanding of Islam.

But we know it's not like that...
At least I know.

So I wanted to shed a light on Islam that hasn't been shed before. And what better way to do that than coupling it with the Top Ten? See, the longer we continue to believe that Christianity is the only way, and Islam is not right, the longer we continue to spin the wonderful cycle of Willie Lynch coming back to life. Because all we've been doin' is separating ourselves — with every little turn and distinction, every category and designation, we continue to separate ourselves from what is truly the goal...

Humanity.

So with that in mind, I wanted to talk about the Ten Commandments and Christian notions and how, interestingly enough, these are quite similar to the Fatihah, Shahadha and notions of Islam...which are also, interestingly enough, quite similar to aspects of Supreme Mathematics amongst the Nation of Gods and Earths. Understand what type of fact-checking situation this lends itself to. And since I'm the type of kat that can't sleep right at night if one day I find out my words and deeds, writings and actions, are not right and exact, everyday has been a constant pursuit of knowledge: the continuous task

2

of stripping and replenishing, destroying only to rebuild, tweaking and twerking, touching up and detailing so dramatically, my brain hurts. And if you knew me, and *my* brain, you'd know what that means...word. But it's critical that it's right, for everybody involved, because a conversation like this has the ability to really do a lot in the climate we presently maintain in, this sick-ass trap I call life. 'Cause the way it works out for me is this—I grew up around a lot of dudes and even went to Sunday school and church with kats that wound up being criminals on many levels. Understand part of it has to do with the environment we've been placed in—but that's different conversation. Christianity just didn't do it for them. And, as we all know, that fast-life we call the life of crime—all that hustlin'—only leads you to one of two places...

One is the cemetery, and really, it's not fair that I've been to more funerals for friends than I have years in age...

The other is jail...*if* one is that lucky...
And really, you tell me what's lucky about jail...

And I've seen kats leave for their jail bids as Christians and come back Muslim or come back God body, and be completely different. They've changed their ways, literally made the one-eighty, and flip scripts in a way that the community they were killing before they left is now the same community they're trying to revive with CPR—hands crossed pumping chest and occasionally yet systematically stopping to breathe into its mouth. They

3

politick with the drug dealers, and not to cop, but instead, to tell them to stop spreading the poison. They poly with the youth, and not to co-sign the "wil' outs" or the "don't snitch" campaigns of absolute stupidity. Instead, they tell them to stop the ignorance, to pick up a book and read, to choose a different option, a different lifestyle. Because indeed, they do have choices.

Now, how do I ignore that? How do I deny that and say it doesn't exist? I don't...

Instead, I live with the words of my brethren and family. One day, Din told me this: He said "...Todd, the way I see it, if you worship a banana...for real sun, if you worship a banana, and that banana keeps you on the straight and narrow...that banana allows you to do good in the world and to live right and just...and it keeps you from approaching me when I'm with my daughters and violating my family...then you know what, you ga'head and rock with that banana, I ain't mad at you..."

Now at the end of the day, how real is that? We so busy runnin' around trying to live out these separations, instead of really living life, respecting how sometimes differences help to serve the purpose of community. Humanity. Living right, together and unified. And really, why wouldn't we all want that? Ain't *that* what it's supposed to be?

...I really thought that's what it was...

So understand that to have these themes runnin' through this novel and these ten torturous stories is not a coincidence or fluke of happenstance. This is what it is for me. Here I am, runnin' around with at least three different sets of universal truths and philosophic virtues on my back, and tryin' to honor each one.

But I haven't even gotten to the stories yet...

And when I get to them, they're all in the hood. You *know* I gotta get the hood right...you crazy?!? These stories, they take place in an environment that resembles my home, my peoples' homes, so I can't not get that right, too. I gotta make sure I give you the way the hood breathes, the way it exists and allows people to begin to exist within it. The same hood that teaches life and death, love and hate, war and peace, and even money and crime. The hood that never sleeps, and teaches people how to talk in a never-ending and ongoing event called slang and vernacular, sentences and conversation...and slows down, but never leaves anything out, never glosses over anything, like jigsaw puzzle pieces used to paint the full picture and make all parts stand whole. So that it never ends in the hard stop given by the English language...instead, it just...breathes...pauses...

"The only time a conversation ends is when a life is taken."

Otherwise, it merely slows down just enough so it continues on and on...the same way three periods called ellipses do...and not for nothin', that's the trinity of my words...

So understand when you pick this up and read, there's gonna be some spots that don't necessarily sit well for the stereotypes and fallacies we've been given. Does that make it any more wrong than your way? Know that you're gonna hit some points where you may really have to let that guard of yours down and walk through the hood for a little second. I know normally you may be scared, but you cool with me today, I'm the direct connect that lends the extended "ghetto pass" to anyone so long as you can say you walkin' with me. And after the hood nods its head, and lets you through its entrance, then you gotta put down the other guard that allows you to say, "...ah, I don't mess with five percenters, they think they God..." or "...nah, them Muslim dudes, I be seeing what they do on the News..."

Leave that home...

What it really comes down to is, you might not mess with the Gods, but if you listen to hip-hop, then you're engaged in what is now mainstream popular culture; with that, understand every time you go to use the word "son" it's not that. It's "sun" my dude—not a degradation, but the utmost form of compliment. I learned that back in '95 when I was told "I call my brother sun 'cause he shines like one." It's not "word is born." It's "word is bond"—'cause your word is your bond, constantly connected to the notion of freedom...something my peoples have been losing for a minute now. Everybody stays talkin' 'bout their God U Nows, their four-pounds and four-powers. Know you get that language from the same Gods and Earths you said a page ago you wasn't messin' with...

...how 'bout *that*, sun...?

That same language and slang you now use as a piece of appropriated popular culture (again, another whole conversation by itself, just ride wit' me here real quick) originated in some of the spots you too scared to go to at night, came from some of the same people you swore up and down you wasn't messin' with. So *now* what you gon' do? Try to flip your slang, change your whole language up, and wait for your peoples and your hood to catch on?

You wouldn't risk that...so instead, leave that home...
...*please*...

And to the youth...my youth that are dyin' everyday out here on these streets, listen yo, for real. You have choices, many of them, most of them you don't even know about yet. They may take work, but the fast-life is not the way to get there. Stop bein' led to believe that bein' stupid is being cool. Stop thinking the way to be hard is to be shot at, or locked up. Stop thinking the fast-life is gonna take you outta here. 'Cause it will take you outta here alright, outta here in a way you just don't want. It'll leave you dead and it has no remorse. And best believe when I tell you it won't shed no tears at your funeral, won't send flowers, cards, or even warm regards...

...it'll just get to the next kat it's gonna eat up and spit out.

7

So how 'bout you take some knowledge real fast...?

Trust me, I won't let you down, believe me when I tell you. If you take this roller coaster ride with me, I will strap you in and take you through it. You get to live at the end and ain't no dumb long lines like at Great Adventure for my bang-out...and that's word!

Just understand I'm bringing you through three different stratospheres, three separate but similar spiritual planes of existence, with a backdrop called the hood. I mean, after all, why have it go down anywhere else? That's where I'm from, that's what made me...and to be honest, I wouldn't have it any other way.

Know what you'll see in this countdown called a novel is how all three of these worlds interact and combine, 'cause contrary to popular belief, the hood lives and breathes, thus these stories do just that. And broken down by the commandments, you'll see seven chapters that deal with the way the world works, how man interacts with man. Then you'll see the way the cerebral works; some things involve the way we interact in life on a daily basis. With that, there are also some things we deal with solely in our mental—our individual brains—in whatever closeness you may have with your designated "Higher Power." That intimacy is not privy to the world for display, that essentially takes place in the mind. I know I'm askin' you to take a real big leap and stretch to do that. It's all good though my dude, you ridin' wit' me. As we say in hip-hop culture, you are now rockin' wit' the best. And not for nothin', my peoples from the hood are wil' smart—sometimes we just tend to focus our energy

8

in directions that may not lead to the right path. That doesn't mean the hood ain't smart…it just means we're not requested to use our brains in this way.

So fear not, I got you…just walk with me…

'Cause at the end of the day, we all know we are supposed to live life right. If anyone has an argument for anything otherwise, I'd really like to know…

…I don't care, but I'd like to know the thinking that paves the path of lunacy…

I share in this torture more than any of you know. Maybe that's just the gift I've been given. It's different than yours. But we all have at least one. I guess this is it for me. I suggest you find yours, instead of bein' so fuckin' busy worried about whether one story I bring to life hits a little too close to home. Why don't you sit down and *read*? After all, it's not about that. It's about the jewels encased in this ink I'm sharing with you.

…for truly, this is my torture…

So this is how I'll sum it up, in one scenario that everyone can see:

Imagine going to the movies, and sneaking into the second one that you didn't pay for. You've sat in the theater and been patient, waiting for the previews to start, but you don't complain, 'cause after all, you did sneak into this one. And now you've been there for the beginning and have gotten into the movie and just as the good part is about to come on, the usher walks down the aisle and informs you that since you don't have a ticket stub, you must leave... "...please come with me..." he says...

And with that, there is no happy ending, there is no sad ending...there is, in fact, no resolution...simply a judgment day song through one-ninth of the greatest of hip-hop...which has fueled this effort for three years of burning...

"...torture...
...torture...
...torture...

y'all nigguhs know..."

Method Man, "Torture"
Tical Part 2: Judgment Day
Def Jam Recordings, 1999

Part II

...and afterwards, while still in His presence,
He gave me instructions as to how to convene in relation
to one another...

Person 1: These days, challenge is all over...
everybody wants to be number one...

Person 2: Heeeuuh...then something must be
cooking...

Person 1: Yes...I was challenged, too...

10—Thou shalt not covet thy neighbour's house, thou shalt not covet thy neighbour's wife, nor his manservant, nor his maidservant, nor his ox, nor his ass, nor any thing that is thy neighbour's.

The Holy Bible, King James Version, Exodus 20:17

Knowledge add Cypher

Supreme Mathematics

"...let me tell you how it's going down/
it's on now/
nigguhs used to love me
now they wanna hate me now/
I'm that same nigguh wit' the Tech
holdin' the spot down/
except I'm pushin' a Lex,
lettin' the top down..."

Big Noyd, "The Learning (Burn)"
Infamy, Loud Records, 2001.

...drugged by envious slugs like a chick slipped wit mickey...

...and Christian had to motivate and make another move up outta illadelph...and while he was more than happy to be on his way home, it was still difficult to go...but he knew he had to... regardless of where he was in the world, he knew there was nothing and no place like home...the Universe entitled through the exclusive stitching on tongues of exclusively classic Nike Air Ones...NYC was the space...and while The Badlands was the origin of his existence, now home took on a new spot...after all, Christian couldn't bear to see in the flesh what was going down in his mom's crib...and besides, there was really no room there for him now for various reasons ...and anyway, thun's tongue was entirely too sharp...Chris, he'd wind up saying something real foul to Jerry and let his words commence the manifestation of physical altercations...and if the hood came up outta him like that right now... "...there's no telling where I might go...what I might do..."...Christian could only imagine, and then apologize for even contemplating something along those lines ...home was now really where his heart was at...Emil had always been close to him...him and Damon were the two brothers Chris never biologically had...that ain't stop nothin' though, 'cause Christian, Emil and Damon was like brothers ...really, like chess pieces labeled Bishop and Q in back-in-the-day attained power and respect through juice formulated as fluid, they were brothers, kin in every sense of the word... and now that it was only them two, that's how Chris looked at eM...

...hopping in the hooptie he had bought Ayesha, because his pockets were pathetically penniless and her car was the epitome of economy on gas, he bounced from the spot with the talking walls and imprints of imperfections he impressed on particular individuals...Chris headed north on the turnpike through Jersey...and bypassing any parts of The Badlands, he floated right out to Gilligan's Island...eM lived out there in a ill crib, the spoils of his sacrifices and successes...and it was all Chris ever dreamed of...he just hadn't gotten there yet...from the fenced-off front, eM's fortress was surrounded by moats of plush lime green lawns guarded by atrocious alligators starring as three ravenous rottweilers that would tear that ass up if the eminent scent of an intruder was not sniffed as recognizable...the plush roots which once lay dead as ashes were now resuscitated, brought back to life...and like the lawns alive again, so too was eM, as he began to grab his life and see the science of the world around him...and with three seclusive stories each bigger than the crib they grew up in together, eM's home was home to Christian...eM had been there for his thunthun...his sunsun...his brother Chris...from day one...it was no wonder why Chris floated straight out there...that was where he could escape the chaos of the world and sort it all out...it was an inescapable time warp...clouded with the haze of greenery and green-boxed squares, there were no confines or restraints...and just like the island Gilligan and his counterparts were trapped on, there was one way in, one way out, and one was stuck if he didn't have a ride to float...and as far as it was, it's location and strategic setting

16

was almost identical to The Badlands...on the way, bangin' eM's new album, Christian couldn't wait to be with his family, his whole clique...primarily his brother...he was most important to him...Christian loved Emil...and unfortunately, eM was the only one who could help him with this situation...

...eM's crib was completely different now, as he had done a lot of work with it...he had been going harder than hard, and anyone or thing in his way of going hard had to be eliminated...straight-up annihilated...for life was entirely too short for the nonsense...but more importantly, eM had already been through the bullshit and dealt with the bullshit...eM had gained his manhood through this...here, Chris would have to lose his...and while everyone thought what Chris had would get him what he wanted, he had all he ever wanted, needed, or could even ask for...now he was here, about to approach eM yet again, because for some strange reason, Christian had spazzed out and given it all up...and yeah, shit was fucked up and not completely his fault, but at the end of the day, Chris couldn't even sleep at night knowing some of the things he had done and some of the shit he had been in and put people through...particularly one individual...the one who murked off on him, methodically masterminding moves on him when his ego would not allow him to see the signs that were ominously evident...here lied the consequences of his own actions, here would lie the torment that had eaten away at him since he thought about maybe picking up the gat and blasting off...after all, he figured there was already a bounty on his head from

17

Ayesha's side...he already had dreams of her Ecuadorian bloodlines stomping him out in the same way his clique got down in The Badlands...he thought back to the day when thirty seconds lasted an infinite eternity, when he was stuck and scrunged up in that small ass pawn shop with his in-lawed brother Osirus who they called Ossie...Chris was shook to death, stuck and fucked like a mark...an easily-catchable-moving-target that stayed stagnant for its capture...and with that, Christian did not want to be anywhere near TwoFifth and Lex, knowing that's where Ayesha's peoples ran...and knowing they were watching-waiting-and-layin' to see a nigguh that looked even remotely like thun...so they could run up spitting gem-star-razor-blades out the mouth, leaving Chris buck-fiftied up, sliced and diced like sautéed onions on the hot-as-a-skillet streets of Harlem world...Chris knew they were sleeping-creepin'-and-crawlin' to catch him in the form of a white lab mouse in the experimental maze of harLEm de español—then air that whole shit out with the hopes that he got caught up in that muthafucka...so what if the rest of the innocent casualties on the block they aired out got hit—

Clearly Christian didn't care when he was buckin' off his emotions at Ayesha—

...why should they care now...?...here, death was wished on that nigguh C, so with that, he had to begin to make a move up outta where he was, because Ayesha's peoples all knew where thun lived...and he knew just as

18

well as she did that she ran wit a clique a killers...so did he...she knew them in the flesh and heard of them in all the songs...the illest killer outta his team wasn't here no more though...so Christian definitely felt hell on earth being a man down...this wasn't Damon's fault though...Deem surely had done everything he could from where he was to prevent this...but there was only so much he could do given Chris and how he was getting down...even Damon ain't know who his brother was...so now, here Chris was with his brother...in a position that every brother goes through with another brother...that's what they are there for...still, it fucked up Christian's development in his own eyes...he just hadn't yet acknowledged it actually brought him full circle to where he needed to be, in this most extreme lesson in patience and humility...the same patience he told Ayesha was a virtue in their early days...like the way her granma, that he had called upon at one point, had told her...the same humility he used to approach Ayesha in those beginning days...from the wake of sunrise...to the slumber of sunset...and back...now corrupted and contorted into something that all the outside authorities changed in their welcoming home of one prodigal daughter, and one rejection of the flock in what could now be considered a wandering and prodigal son, here Christian was to deal with this element he did not want to face...he knew he had to do it on his own...yet he couldn't do it all by himself...he had to ask someone..."...a closed mouth doesn't get fed..."...and eM was really the only one he could ask who could understand, ask no questions, and tell no lies...Chris was trying to get there...he just hadn't yet...but he was

19

working on it…

…Christian got up outta the seat he always rocked in at eM's house, right there near the window, and then descended down to the dungeon deemed eM's basement, the studio eM built for his work…he had everything he needed right in the comfort and privacy of his own home…the truth was eM had it like this because he stayed going hard, all day e'ryday…thun did not stop and would not slow down as he lived what Chris knew in his heart and wrote on the page all day…that time waits for no man…yeah, damn right eM was hustling…hustling at this music game trying to get it to the point where he would be alright, and his little thun would be set…every minute was spent getting that shit, only because he was getting these beats right in his dream of living life…doing what he loved to do…Chris wasn't there…and this trip down the cold concrete stairs would strangle Christian's coming of age in the form of upliftment…this was something he didn't know right then…and so instead, all he could think of was what was going down and how it had come down to this…he was fucked up with the fact that this was the situation at hand, yet and still, he continued down the stairs down to the door and down in the chair…eM had the music screeching, slicing the waves of sound so that any and every eardrum would vibrate until the heart felt what he was feeling…here was his dream, and every minute of the day thun went hard…Chris, he had fallen off, not going hard at anything, becoming completely complacent in the life he lived that was clearly inadequate…after all, Ayesha did skate, didn't she…?…he was on the road to recovery, but he was stuck in a way that cracked his cranium and shattered what ego he did have...and he had entirely too much of it...so now, as he tried to shed it and walk in a different direction from where he had been, he figured he had a lot to do in order to get to a point where this situation would not be a possibility anymore...however, Chris was here because of all he had done...and now...here was, unbeknownst to him, yet another that he would have to contend with..."as if I haven't been doin' enough fightin' already..." he thought to himself, as he let his emotions feel what eM was talking about in four bars by fours bars...this was eM's way of life, it led him out of life's confines and gave him freedom...Christian couldn't even see what his was now...now that Ayesha was gone...

"...how much you need thunthun..."
...and when he asked eM what he had to, eM told him not to worry about it..."...everything happens for a reason..." was what eM told Christian...and they both knew it was true, for they both said it constantly...their thinking was so succinct in certain scenarios, one would think that mentally their brilliance was twinned on some level...that's 'cause when they were younger, they ran around together all day e'ryday, like clockwork...they grew up like that...and they kept going with each other until it was time for them to take different directions...still they approached each obstacle with the same mentality...because they both came up the same...eM had it all, ready to do what society told them the dream was...

21

"...it's gonna cost like eleven or twelve hundred...but if you could give me like six or seven..."

...and here Christian was with nothing, as he had followed a different dream towards symbols that would not take away his blackness...he wasn't supposed to do what he had done...and here he was, paying for it on many levels...he had hit bottom when Ayesha bounced...now he needed a helping hand in just getting back to ground level...for she had always been that hand for him...for a long time...and for some reason, the last time, he rejected that only hand, bit the only one that would feed him...literally...mentally...physically...emotionally...she was everything to him, his world, his whole existence...and now, in trying to find out how to exist on his own again yet in a way never known to him from any of his other exploits, endeavors and encounters in life and love, eM's hand was the only one that could pull him up...this was where it would go down...

"...hold on for a minute...I'll be back..."

...and Chris was happy for eM yet hurt by how he could just make moves when he wanted...fiscal constraints were not an issue to or for him...but Chris knew his whole crew and he realized that Emil was the one who had gone the hardest at what he wanted to do for life... "...I'm just coming to the realization..." Christian thought to himself, knowing full well that even though he was going hard right now, he hadn't been in a minute...that was the

22

problem...and he went hard at something that he inevitably gave up, so really what was the point of going hard if that's what Chris was gonna do...?...but even eM had been at a point where it all fell and he had to pick all the pieces back up again and keep it moving...and next time go even harder than the last because it was exactly as he said, for life...Christian had it tatted on him...titled it and all that...and still, here he was...maybe if he would have been going hard on all levels in the first place, he wouldn't be in this situation with his brother...because now, Christian looked at his manhood in an entirely different way, and being aware of his actions based on hindsight, through the negative way of life he had created for himself and another, he had to refine his conception and manifestations of strength...and instead of perpetuating incarceration, he needed to live granting freedom through the fairness of the *God* he was working with...he had constructed only to demolish...now he had to create his own genesis, in a dawn giving birth and being born into the position of intellect of his clique...it just so happened that the way he was going and the way his clique was going were two different paths and his didn't lead to what any of his peoples would have as quickly...but he hadn't been going hard...and eM, he stayed going hard all day e'ryday...it took him awhile to get to where he was...eM wasn't playing, though...on any level...part of Christian's problem was once he got what he had, he played around with it, on some real-live thinking he was completely-invincible shit...that's what got the rush on, and got him in the situation he was in now, forcing back the thought of committing such a sinful act...at this point, he had been back and forth and back again...and as he assessed his newfound spirit, he knew he was not supposed to let his mind and person go here...for he had been in many an instance, and understood this most final of numbers, listening to Him as He had told Christian through Word and Action that he was not supposed to feel this type of way...the last command He gave to the world and His people...yet at the same time, he really was down right now...and he could begin to feel the hate flowing in his blood, because he had to come to this kat who was on top, swallowing his manhood because he wasn't up...Chris was on his way though...and his torture was that he wasn't getting there fast enough for his own liking...but he had been down before...and even then, when he was down, he had Ayesha right there with him, so it seemed as if it was all good...he knew how high the stakes were, even eM had told Christian what time it was...told him he wasn't supposed to go at it like that, chill out and let the shit work itself out...but since Christian had an 11x14 piece of paper, on some level, nobody could tell him shit...after all, his bloodlines were dissimilar, but his heart, soul and essence was just like his blood brother...and just as eM was always right, so was Christian...he was the dude they always directed the questions at, because *he* was the smartest kat of them all, he was the one that did it...but sometimes, even Chris didn't have all the answers to all the questions...maybe if he had done some things the way his peoples had, he wouldn't be here having this conversation with eM...yet

24

again...that was what r.i.p.ped thun heart out...'cause eM knew what time it was immediately when it happened...and no matter what, he was gonna be there because he knew his brother was trying to do shit the right way, and he would help Chris in any way he could...even lay down his life for him if it came down to it...and Christian felt the same way...but something about it took his manhood away, because he knew eM would never come to him like this...Christian would do anything he could, he was always there, no matter what he could do...but he ain't have it like that, so if eM was fucked up and needed dough to make any type of move, what use would Christian actually be...?...he didn't have it poppin' like that...that's what hurt the most, for what if it did go down like that...?...it made Chris think of all the time he wasted...he hadn't been going hard and was blaming it on any and everything except for his own self...here he was going against his own grain, so that now, he was stuck...and as much as he had to make moves he couldn't...last time he had to really make a move, eM looked out for him...eM always looked out for him...he loved eM for that because Emil was his brother...Christian looked at eM like that...they grew up from the dirt together...from first grade recess sessions actin' bent singing "how dry I am"...now they were both dry...he had asked eM to hold himself down and look out for himself when no one else would...and eM, eM told Christian that he should do the same, only at a different time...eM knew what Christian felt was real, but he just wanted his brother to be careful, because everything had

25

been lost, and the stakes were indeed mad high...this was the type of shit eM could do...but Christian, eM knew just as well as Chris that his brother couldn't...Christian, he had too much to lose...and with everything eM had, he tried to protect and safeguard his brother's safety... because his brother had done it right, and in a way that no one else in the crew had...and just as eM kept platinum plaques that Christian admired with awe, eM respected and cherished his brother's academic accomplishments ...he was that smart nigguh...and he did have too much to lose...yet and still, Christian did what he did because he was going hard then...and he wasn't trying to hear nothing else...but then he stopped going hard in the right way but in the most vile of ways, so that he was actually shittin' on the fact that the stakes were as high as they were...it was just that serious...Chris knew life could not be a trip one moved oblivious through...and because he had, here he was in this final of tests, most vicious of toils, most terrible of snares...because here, he had to ask, nothing could go down without the help he needed from his brother...and Christian was humble...something he had not been when this situation came to a head right ahead of him as he instead looked behind, backing down a street he was supposed to be driving straight through ...yes, Christian had flipped scripts, slammed on the brakes, thrown it retroactively in reverse, and backed down that shit when he was supposed to be moving ahead...that's what it seemed like in real life...Christian had to put the pieces back together...and eM was there for him on all levels...funny thing was, eM was always there,

26

through Christian's triumphs and defeats...as Chris was for eM's pitfalls and ascents...Chris always hoped they would meet at the top, click flute glasses full of champagne and toast, celebrating success...but he hadn't completed his part of the bargain...and as the bitch was not Ayesha, but what she so desperately described as hindsight which hit him hundredfold for forgetting how ill it could be, Christian was now stuck to *build* back up from the destruction of his lifestyle with his other half—his heart and his wifey—who had always tried to grow with him, together...yet he was here to do it alone with the awareness of his own actions...the same actions that led him here...he needed help in this spot from his brother in the *cypher* he moved with..."...how did it get to this...?..." Christian thought...and he realized that he hadn't been going hard...but he would now...

"...here...don't wet it...it ain't nothin'..."

...eM gave Chris fifteen green swollen-faced Benjamins...double what he asked for and more than he said he needed—just in case...and like Esau graciously giving up his birthright in being stuck by Jacob, when eM did this, Christian's manhood was mysteriously taken...and he knew the time would soon come where he would have to pursue in a way like no other...he knew at one point he would have to begin chasing Ayesha...

...but it was only him now...at the same time, it was only them two left, on some man to man shit...and while he didn't know how or why, the gore and gritty grunge and grime of the greenest of envious sins challenged his brain and his rejuvenated and renovated modus operandi with life in a way he couldn't understand...for he loved his brother...but now it was his only...

...and so without question, eM would hold his brother down, 'cause he loved him too...last time he told Christian he knew he was trying to do things right, and he was better than a lot a nigguhs that was coming at him sideways with a lot of bullshit schemes and snake plans to get at him..."...you family...and I know you trying to do shit the right way...we all fuck up sometimes though...it ain't nufin..."...but as Chris motioned to take the money from this man's hand, he stopped...for in a split second, he also wanted to bite it off, even though it was the only hand that could or did feed him...and Christian knew here he had to trust in his brother...and on some level, *acknowledge* his status in this *cypher*...for he would be damned if he did not...yet, he'd be damned if he did...take it...

28

...and as he tried with all he had to push this emotion out of his head, this was his torture...

...and as the tear fell from his eye he watched his brother go back to work at the beats...and as the volume increased, so did the pain in Christian's heart...so did the fight to ward off his ego in his attempt to exist in humility...for it was not him at all...instead, it was in fact, the ego which tried to penetrate his person and circulate hate in his blood to his heart...and here, this was where Christian's new war would begin...

...within himself...

...and he wondered about this most as his torture...

...and he wondered when it would end...

9—Thou shalt not bear false witness against thy neighbour.

The Holy Bible, King James Version, Exodus 20:16

9—Born

Supreme Mathematics

"...let's talk about lane switchin'...

And without question, thun was on the run...and he had to make moves because the name the streets and the hood gave him was catchin' up to him in a way like no other...and in the same way the world loved freedom, so too did he...but time was running out for him...on a lot of levels...it was here, though, that his run would soon end...for years and years, Emil tried to tell thun not to do some of the shit he was doing...Deem was Emil's bloodline...just as he was with his brother Christian...and since it was all in the fam'ly, a equaled b which also equaled c...for Deem, he was right when he was right...Deem was even right when he was wrong...and they ain't call thun Deem for nothing...'cause if someone was fucking with him in the wrong way, thun would pull out his flamer and burn somethin'...peel out the banger and blast somethin'...cock back the gat and buck somethin'...for real for real, shit be that real sun...

...even Emil was concerned about his crazed kin, sharing his sentiments when he saw Christian that day in the summertime...Deem didn't know too much about his pops...he was gone...all he really knew about his father was they shared the same name in the form of a government...yet each rocked with a different form of it, so that his absentee father was the first one, and next came Damon Christian Junior...but as the cold world raised this young man to his prime ahead of his time, he was given a new name...so that after Junior, it was Damon...now, in a new day and age, as another era dawned on the hood, on

33

eM, and on his peoples, Damon turned to Deem...thun was calm and quiet, cool and collected...but if you crossed him, he'd cross over to somewhere else and shift deviant, treacherous...diabolical, he'd demonstrate the essence of demonic downfalls upon his deceased enemy...that is, by the time he finished...his peoples could tell it was coming when his eyes twitched devilish, opening and turning red like a Demon...so they called him Deem...and a killer he was...but he only unleashed that part of his persona if he had to, only if a person truly deserved it...for he wasn't one of these kats out in the world who felt that manhood was gained by bucking and busting a gun...nah...if Deem was coming, it only meant that someone had it coming because of an action which led to some real foul shit...he rolled with God in that way, and God held him down, almost as if Deem was like God's personal grim reaper...the heavensent angel of death...

...as eM walked up through the block to see Christian walking in his direction, he gave his brother a strong pound and mad love...last time he saw his older brother was during vacation, and as Christian graduated from high school and was on his way to college, he had to check his peoples in the hood for a reality check that really wasn't one for Christian right then...for eM, Emil was hustling hard in the streets to make his music game happen...but Chris, thun was moving through a white high school on his way to a white college in the white snowcapped mountains in a car with a white bitch that he called the love of his life, but was only fuckin' with him so that when they got back to Beantown, she could tell her

34

friends how real both he, and subsequently, she, was because she was in the hood with her black man, and was in the hood meetin' his black brother...so infatuated with the notion of blackness, that when it came back to strike her, she tried to shit on the persona that captivated her energy in the first place...

"...yo sun, Deem on the block..." eM said to Christian...

"...word...how dun doing..."

"...yo, I can't even fuck wit sun right now...he crazy yo...I don't know where thun head's at right now..." eM replied, with a serious look of concern on his face, one that Christian had never seen on Emil's face before...Christian didn't know that Deem was walking around with a bullet in his head and his leg from when this kornball kat in the hood tried to front and buck at him...sending off bullets meant to git him...and once he regained consciousness, he checked himself right outta that hospital as quick as he was involuntarily checked in, knowing he had to show these other asscheek-nigguhs in the hood just how thoro he actually was...little did Deem know how much of a nuisance this muthafucka would be to his existence...

...and they walked together to the car so Christian could introduce eM-the-star to this white woman who would never know eM-the-brother-of-his...

"...she white sun..." Christian said to eM...

"...you know I don't give a fuck...I knew she was white *anyway* thun-thun..."...eM said to his brother, as

35

they both laughed, feeling good about seeing each other for the first time in a little while, what the hood called a hot minute…eM approached the passenger side of the car on his best behavior…and no sooner than Christian introduced this woman to eM, had he told her to chill, lock the doors and wait…"…I'll be right back…" Christian said, knowing meeting eM with her on the outskirts of the hood was one thing…walking through the block with this white bitch, though…that was something else…and he had to go see his namesake…

Christian and Emil scurried away from the car and into the abyss of The Badlands, through the 14th side to the other end of the block entitled 21st street…it was here that Christian would see Deem…and on this hot-ass summer day, Deem was wearing a hoodie with army fatigues, thinking his disguise would cloak and cloud his ultimate demise, hiding from the police on all levels…

"…what up dundun…" Christian said to Deem, who looked at him real strange, but still showed him love…

"…what up cousin…" Deem replied, giving his namesake a paranoid pound and hug, making sure police was not mappin' out his motions…

"…you aight sun…?…" Christian said to his brother, while eM played the background, not wanting to approach his now-deranged kin…

"…yeah sun…I'm cool thun…how you…you still in school…?…" and just as Christian was about to respond,

"…yeah…I'm goin–"

"Yo, I'm out thunthun…one…" Deem said, giving Christian a pound, pulling the hood over his head, and making a quick move further into the abyss as the blue and white vehicle turned the corner to make its rounds…

"…Be safe dun…" was all Christian could say as his brother disappeared into The Badlands' thin air…he turned to look at Emil, who just shook his head…

"…c'mon sunsun…I'll walk you back to the car…you know how nigguhs out here is…you can't leave that white bitch in the car like that forever…"

"…word, you right…" Christian said, as they both broke into laughter again, turned around and walked back through the block so Christian could get back to the car…and for the first time in a long time, the hood did check Christian into Hotel Reality, Room 101…'cause right then, he forgot about the passenger which had been his priority…his head was now stuck on his namesake…

"…why the fuck is dun on the run…" he thought to himself…

…and it would only come to Christian a month or two later, when he was home for a vacation from school…for when he was alone in his mom's crib, the doorbell and pounding awakened him from his slumber…and when he answered the door, barely awake in his boxers, he was asked if Christian was home…and he replied…

"…that's me…"

...and what was once two people instantaneously turned to ten, each with two gats...so now, Christian only saw the pipes of twenty gats as he speechlessly uttered his last name...

"...I'm just home from college..."

...and the gats which were once raised, lowered like a drawbridge, letting him back into life...which he lost for a few seconds but now his heart was beating again...

"...no...my brother is not here...and to be honest...after that shit you just fuckin' did to me, I wouldn't fuckin' tell you pigs if he was...!"
Christian, now gaining what little heart he did have back, slammed the door in police face harder than they all pulled out on him...

"...damn cousin...is it really that bad...?...be safe sun...please..." Christian said to himself, praying for his namesake...

...in the name of Allah...The Beneficent...The Merciful...

...and it would be months later before Deem was finally caught...and when he went to jail, things began to change for thun...he began to reflect on the things he had done, all his past actions both spoken in his word and withheld in his heart...he thought about where he was and where he was going...he reviewed his relationship with

God, or the lack thereof...and in the bingbing Deem found a new thingthing that preserved his life much better than the gun Nas talked about having...and after taking the Shahadha and proclaiming Allah as his one and only God, he changed his name and life as Allah gave him a new outlook...and thus came Abdullah Zahir, the shining, radiant and elevated servant of God...Sunni in every sense of the word...and walking a freshly paved path with Allah, The Most Righteous helped Abdullah to figure out where he had been, where he was going, and how he was to get there...and it was here where Abdullah Zahir would learn how to walk in the path of The Almighty God...walk hand in hand with Allah...and now, incarcerated within inverted mirrors, Deem flipped letters to Ab, and thus was left to reflect right on instances past...it was here that Ab became informed of his expressions and actions through his perception in his self-reflection...it was in this physical state of animalistic entrapment called incarceration that Abdullah Zahir's daily experience came clear to him, how he was trapped in a rut that inhibited him yet orchestrated his own spiritual freedom, freedom through his new name...and it was in this place and space that Abdullah learned the ninety-nine names of Allah, in order to gain strength through this snare that would inevitably give him purity...and with *Al-Haqq*, he found his balance given to him by *The Truth*...it was through *Al-Rabb* that Abdullah Zahir manifested his proper place through *The Lord*...and here with *Al-Tawwab*, he did not fear either the act of constructing or dismantling, as he now moved with *He Who is Near to His Creation*...and escaping the sick trap of

39

this world by elevating his mental up and out of his physical into a place and space with his new God, his Only God, his *Al-Karim — The Most Noble — The Generous Giver* gave the freedom of life to Abdullah, so that as long as His most faithful follower moved with Him, He would indeed show him why He was called *Al-Qahhar* and *Al-Majid...The Invincible, The Victorious*...and finally, *The Glorious*...and in this most swiftest of name changes, he would soon be forced to realize exactly how snakes slithered through the grass, side winding while switchin' lanes...

...all praise is due to Allah...The Lord of the World...

...yet and still, he would rebuke his government, he would rebuke the streets...for here, Abdullah was left to reconcile and destroy whatever led him here with Allah...coming together to bring a new birth and genesis to Ab...he now only had to persevere through the long days, longer nights, and the four-by-four cell that held him...it no longer did that though...for now, it was indeed Abdullah who was moving with God, The One and Only...Allah...

"...Allah U-Akbar..." would be his chant, shortly after he methodically unraveled the prayer rug, and descending on bended knees, bowed in worship, giving praises to The Most High...similar to the way his man rhyming from his clique would do, right after spreading his wings, waking up to a new day in days to come...Ab would not be here for that, but he would be...just not in the way they all thought...

...the important thing though, was that he was not one to be caged up...and so it was through his walk, travels and journeys with Allah in prayer five times a day that he began to understand how he was to escape...for Allah would elevate Abdullah's mental from the prison of the physical...so that his spirit and his essence would not only rise like Maya from the cell, but would rise like baking dough from his own physical dimensions...so that while Ab was there in the flesh, through lock-down and roll-call, in the yard and in the shower, Abdullah Zahir's essence was now with Allah...and it was his God Allah who ultimately bestowed his name that would help him to fulfill it, elevate up outta the physical constraints of his body...up outta the physical constraints of the jail cell...up outta the physical constraints of the bars and the ten foot high gates...up above the barbed-wired tips and up above the sky that always wanted to pull him back down through gravity...Abdullah had escaped all that...it was only Deem that was stuck to walk the grounds of the Island of Rikers...

...The Beneficent...The Merciful...Master of the Day of Judgment...

...and once he reached this most opulent form of utopia with Allah, he never wanted to return...nor did he have to...for it would truly be his demise...but both he and Allah knew he would have to in order to return to where he was in the present moment of that time...similar to drawing parallels towards Christianity, for even God

41

knew He would have to let His Only Begotten go to come back in the most torturous of ways...and amidst the turmoil, chaos and mayhem that surrounded his brother Emil on the outside, Ab knew how important it was for him to be back in the world again...because he knew how vulnerable his brother was to the sickness of his surroundings...and so through Allah, Abdullah had to construct a plan in order to return to the world...in the meantime, here he must stay with Allah in order to remedy and rectify that which he was accused of...for here was Abdullah Zahir's torment, his anguish and agony...for only he and Allah truly knew the meaning in his name...now Ab had to speak even the unspoken with Allah, The All-Knowing...

...and while the world thought Ab was in the physical, succumbing to the elements of jailhood vices, they did not know that Abdullah was actually floating in the spiritual...in the same way he now did...for it was merely his inverted name that left him in the form of a physical presence day in and day out...suiting himself up for his trial everyday...he had already escaped, though...and here, Ab was looking at this situation from on high, knowing that with Allah, there was no way Abdullah Zahir's name would not be cleared...and everyday, like clockwork, Abdullah would pray...the early morning Fajar before the sun rose...the Zoohar which usually came before or at the beginning of trial...quietly to himself during the trial...for God said that it was not the one who prayed as a show and spectacle for the world...but instead

42

the one who would pray in the most unorthodox of locations and the most secret of times...and so, he would pray the Asar as the trial dwindled into the afternoon, while no one knew...and then after trial and dinner, his Maghrib prayer was performed...and upon the infamous call of "lights out" Abdullah gave thanks in the form of the Isha...and days turned into weeks...still, Abdullah Zahir was with The Most Righteous...and prayed to Him knowing his faith would give birth to his freedom...but there was only one complication...for in this trial, there was only one that the DA held all faith in and looked to in order to keep Abdullah trapped in the physical confines of the cage...and for the life of them all—his friends, his family, and even all his peoples in the hood—no one knew why the District Attorney was not worried about this case...for the prosecution acted as if they had Abdullah Zahir in the bag like the cat they would not let out...and here, weeks would turn into months...and with that, it was only a matter of time before the DA had to let the world know what the secret weapon was...still Ab prayed...and still the prosecution accused...and still the defense defended to the utmost in making Abdullah's freedom be brought to life yet again...

...for in this situation, there were many words spoken and unspoken...the words that were necessary, however, for the DA to make this trial a wrap were the words necessary from Deem explaining how he killed...however, Deem was nowhere to be found...instead, Ab stood in his place...a righteous man...a righteous man who had already been judged by The Most Righteous...and with

43

that, all of these worldly proceedings meant absolutely nothing to him, as he had already been absolutely absolved...and for the prosecution to get Abdullah Zahir to snitch on Deem was an impossibility, for they knew not of one another...and within his understanding of Sunni notions, even Ab followed this ninth code of God...the everlasting code of the streets...for he would not in any way, shape or form be the witness bearing false words against his own neighbor, his own self...

...the question now was, who would be this person ...and that was a question that only the DA had the answer to...

...Thee do we serve...and Thee do we beseech for help...

...and as months turned into more months, the time would draw nigh, and the DA was all but forced to bring on the star of the show...and with this, just like Tupac, all eyes were on this kat who miraculously appeared out of the woodwork no one knew about...and as this time came to pass, it was evident that any and everybody wanted to know exactly who the prosecution was saving as the best for last...see, everyone in the hood at this point knew how close Deem was to coming home...the case had not gone well thus far, with witnesses not only switching up stories and affidavit-ted accounts, but as well, people who were in groups began to testify and see many different things, so by the time the DA needed the star witness, the prosecution hoped that would be enough, for the rest of the case had pretty much been shot out of the water...

...still through all of this, Abdullah Zahir prayed before...and during...and after trial...

...in addition to the other two times a day to complete his prayer cypher...and most times, even more than five...to The Most Powerful...The Most High Exalted...

...and it got to the point where Emil, Paul Michael, Ron, and Emil's mom Natalie were all sitting there in the courtroom, trying to figure out who could have actually seen the whole shit transpire...for none of them had, not from start to end...nor did Abdullah talk to them about a single part of it...he had already made peace with Allah on that subject...for Deem, however, this would be his torture...for never once did he say a word about what happened...so that no matter whether the authorities, his peoples in the hood, and even his lawyer thought he was wrong, here he stood right...for even Deem knew the importance of not snitching on himself...and Ab would participate in nothing like this...

...and now, the time had come where they would be forced to behold that which the DA had held for so long...

"...the Prosecution calls..."

...and as the lawyer accusing Abdullah continued his sentence, naming the name of the secret weapon, the star

45

of this absurd sideshow, they all realized what was going down now...

Abdullah's lawyer kept his poker-face, as he always did...but very slowly and subtly looked back at Emil...this was only after him and Ab looked at one another...no words needed to be exchanged...

...and all Abdullah could think was that if he hadn't snitched on Deem, how could this kat do it...?...

...eM was awestruck, eyes wide open after being wide shut for months on end...Emil looked at his man Ron, who shook his head, unable to speak...Paul Michael, his mouth was wide open...eM turned to look at him...

"...who the fuck you wit...?..." Paul Michael whispered softly, knowing that this wasn't supposed to happen...and right here, this was where eM could not believe the science of life, for this math did not add up for him in any way...he looked at his brother, sitting next to the lawyer...and when their eyes met, eM knew but could not bear to continue to look...for never once did eM see this coming...nor did Ab...but Deem knew...

...and now, eM looked right up on the stand...and as his eyes met this masked crusader whose identity was now revealed, it was Emil's stare that dropped the temperature in the courtroom by fifty degrees...eM couldn't believe it...he thought this was his man... "...this fuckin' nigguh..." eM said to himself... "...I put this muthafucka on sun..." eM whispered, as his moms slapped him in the arm for blaspheming in the courtroom...but here eM was

46

stuck...all he could do was imagine the eyes of this nigguh he thought he really knew...they lived in the same hood...on the same block...the same building even...for about twenty years... "...the nerve of this muthafucka..." eM thought...he had known him for years, for at least two decades...and eM, when he got on top, he thought it was his man he was puttin' onto the record game, not this snake-ass-bastard, who demonstrated just how close him and eM were...for here he sat, with heart enough to point...and not even point at Abdullah Zahir, the righteous servant of God who he knew not, but instead, point at Deem—the man he knew would kill him if he made it out of the courtroom past eM and his clique who all ice-grilled the stand now, letting this bitch-ass-nigguh know that they never wished death...unless they really had to...right then, the witness saw eM close his eyes for a few seconds, wishing with all the might he could muster in his body...

...and when he opened them, his lids arose with his pupils staring dead in the heart of this canary who was now a dead man walking...eM had this muthafuckin' snitch's heart in his hand...

...keep us on the right path...the path of those whom thou has bestowed favors...

"…leave it…"

…those were the words of the radiant and elevated servant of God whose reputation and freedom now rested in the hands of this kat, the right hand man of the asscheeks-nigguh who shot Deem in the head and leg…and it was right here where Abdullah would be put to the ultimate test by the Compeller he worshipped…for Deem, he would have risen from his chair in his jailhouse-rock jumpsuit and somehow pulled out and laid this kat to rest, taking not only the charges he was on trial for, but a new charge with a courtroom full of witnesses to this premeditated murder in the first degree…

…but in the chair next to the lawyer sat the man that The God Allah was working with…

…and so, what would Ab do…?

…for here, he sat righteous, right in the forefront…backed by his whole clique, a crew of chill-out kats who would quickly turn to killers if Deem wasn't gonna kill this nigguh…

…and this was the point at which Ab truly had to decide between his rebirth, as Abdullah Zahir, walking hand in hand with Allah…

…not the path of those whom thy wrath…

...or Deem, walking as man with the gat in hand, cocked back and ready to rock...

...has brought down...

...and now, it was to go down...

"...do you swear to tell the truth..."

...he heard the words as he closed his eyes...

"...the whole truth..."

...he opened both hands, palms upright...

"...and nothing but the truth..."

...and bowed his head...

"…so help you God…?…"

…and softly he spoke…

…for his clique stayed poised behind him…
…ready for the word…
…from the only one who could decide what exactly his
torture would be…

"…I do…"

…nor those who go astray…

"…Allah U-Akbar…"

50

8—Thou shalt not steal.

The Holy Bible, King James Version, Exodus 20:15

8—Build or Destroy

Supreme Mathematics

**...sometimes I feel I gotta...
...sometimes I feel I gotta...
GET-A-WAY
From these streets like a fiend from crack/
they pullin' me back/
that's real...**

Havoc of Mobb Deep, "Getaway"
Infamy, Loud Records, 2001.

...That's the Set-Up Right There...

It was real in the streets of Rensselaer Badlands Houses...a surreal happenstance of subhuman lifestyles and conditions, it was colder than the world GZA spoke of...frigid as the bergs of Antarctica, brisk as the New England breeze that blew early fall mornings, lifting the lifeless limbs of dead colored leaves into a subtle swirling sandstorm...this was the hood he lived in...

Emil was a quiet-type character, a chill-out kat, coming up in a world he never thought could consume him...he got respect in his hood from all the natives, from the hardrocks and hustlas to the stickup kids and conflicted crackheads, characters who all had supporting roles in this motion picture called life...Emil had a life much different than those around him, even though the elements rang the truth in the same way it had for all his friends...'cause in the hood, the broken home from failed nuclear experiments was not the exception, but rather the norm...he lived right there in the middle of the block, his apartment windows looking right out over the basketball courts where the Mr. Everything tournaments jumped off every summer...he remembered growing up and seeing MC Shan and Marley Marl walk through the block on the regular...they knew him as that little wild-child, climbing out the window of his four-story apartment to sneak out to the River Park jams...he wanted to rhyme...and he was gonna be a rapper no matter what...now, at the age of 17, he was going at his dream harder than hard...nothing would stop him from getting that record deal, reaching the level of musician...in the meantime, until his rap dreams jumped off, he would have to deal with the reality of The Badlands that led him to always wear the black Champion hoodie underneath his black certified army jacket...as the sun began to rise, he walked outta his building and began the treacherous day that every sunrise would bring...

"Ay yo eM, what up thun..."

In this hood, everybody called their friends thun...either thun or sun...similar to the faithful definition Method Man would later give to the world in the chorus of a song explaining "I call my brother sun 'cause he shines like one..."...it just so happened that in this hood, they had gotten to the description first and ran with it, creating a whole new dialect through rhyme and reason...

"...What up E..."

eM yelled back at his man who he could tell had been out pulling yet another all-nighter on the streets to get that white sheetrock from out the salt mines and into the poisoned populous, which included eM's moms and pops...eM never knew his father...he only heard rumors about who he *might* be and how stuck he was in the salt mines, compliments of his man Eddy...sometimes, eM would chill with Eddy who played the role of Badlands' finest ghetto alchemist...turning white pebbles to gold ex-spendable in the form of green...Emil wasn't messin' with him last night though, he had to make moves today...he took a minor detour through the court, shook his man's

54

hand and gave him love in the form of a hug right there near the benches which were the 18-and-under-bar-n-grill on his block...and as they hugged, Emil's chest was poked by the heavy Cuban-link-cable dangling around Eddy's neck...

"What happened last night sun...where you was at...?"

"Yo, I had to write some shit, thunthun, you know how that go...I see you got new jewels thun..."

"Just yesterday right off the Plaza...You know it ain't nuffin' sun...long as I got this rock, I got the whole block, bee, for real..."

Emil admired the chain that descended at least forty inches from the top of Eddy's neck to the bottom of his belly button...and from there, was the crazy Mother-and-Child-Jesus piece...and Emil realized he had been poked by the chilly ice stuck in the halo of the Mother Mary...eM held the hovering piece in his hand, weighing it to check the density that hit his hand heavily...this get-up was not hollow...

"What up wit'chu sun...?" Eddy asked Emil, hoping he may be able to convince eM to chill as he continued his street-corner crack sales...

"I'm out to school yo...I'll be back out here later on though..."

"I feel you Emil...handle ya' b.i., I'ma be right here when you get back...aight..."

"Aight then...Peace..." eM started walking again as he held his two fingers up, outstretched in a sign that reflected his outgoing words...

Walking quickly as he always had, Emil dipped through the block, crossed the street, and floated up the next two blocks...he had to take the train right off the Plaza into Manhattan to go to school...and while most lived their alter egos in the form of dreams, he lived his dream...his life was the alter ego...here, he was studying to be an architect...and he was a talented artist, whether with pencil or chalk, pen or even paintbrush, whose ear and eye were aesthetically exquisite...he did not realize how his artisanry would later lead to his artistic development elsewhere...he had gotten it from his pops, who had been a painter but never quite finished his classes due to the irony of unresolved issues...he knew his man Eddy was real cool with his pops, something he did not like in the least...because E *was* an alchemist, but what Emil couldn't deal with was even part of his own life was always turned to gold by the elemental shapeshifter...that made things what they were right now, so he would keep it moving and try to think of the next best topic, like how his debut album would blow off the charts once he got his record deal...in the meantime, he floated to the N train, Manhattan-bound, in order to get to school...

And while there, he did his usual thing...caught up with his peoples, checked out his first two classes of the day, and then roamed the halls...he would go to his architecture class, but no one in the house ever had the money for him to get the art supplies he needed to maintain this love of his...and because he knew it wasn't that they didn't have it, but they spent it elsewhere, his love began to vanish into thin air, leaving a void partially filled by his desire to rock the crowd...the space left was soon to be conflicted in ways he never considered...

By lunchtime, he was long gone from school, slumped down in the seat of the 5 train on the way to his man's crib in Gun Hill Houses...thun had the studio in his bedroom out there, and he would go day in and day out to write songs and make a demo he would always shop...waiting on the train to get close to his stop, he remembered episodes outside of the record label offices...any and every artist who passed, he would beat them in the head senseless...

"Yo, listen to my rhymes...Yo please just check this right here sunsun, this is that shit for real for real..."

And while he was a little thun, he came at kats with the intensity of a big brash bully...he had an energy and determination that struck every one of the rappers who saw him, listened to him shortly, and then passed him on the way into the building to handle the business end, whether it be picking up checks or dropping off the tape of that song they did last night in the studio for the new album...

"Stay at it shorty, you aight...You gon' make it yo..." were the words that always came to eM as he continued his street-corner campaign to be voted next best artist signed to x-y-z label...and no matter how long it would take, he would make it...

The muffled sound of the conductor through the loud speaker let eM know he had made it to his stop, and with that, he. wiped his eyes and stretched as he got up and walked off the train, through the platform, around and down the stairs...walking these streets, he felt like he was

57

in a completely different world, but it was funny how every hood was pretty much the same...same ole politics, same ole laws, but most importantly, the same ole street codes strictly adhered to by the grimiest of gangsters...eM was no different, and he obeyed those codes to the utmost...he always thought it was the sheisty snitch with the loose lips that would ultimately sink the damn ship...and eM would under no circumstances be victim to any titanic-like motions from anyone he rocked with...

eM chilled in the studio for awhile...today, he was just focused on writing...he wasn't gonna lay any vocals down, he wasn't gonna work on the material that needed polishing and cleaning up...instead, he just wanted an ill beat so he could write, writerightritewrightwrite...that was his motto and focus for the day...right now, he had other things on his mind he had to think about...shit was getting drastic in his hood and he tried to get as much of it out on the page as he wrote a story-rhyme today...and it was an interesting story he didn't see coming to life and appropriating that of the author's...eM pulled the strings with the words stuck in his curly-q-cursive that was completely confined to the area of a millimeter above and below the blue stripes he wrote between...and he performed his usual writing routine, curled at the back sitting on the bed, elbows resting upon his knees so he could have the perfect angle to write in his composition book...eM's focus was too intense even for his producer, for he couldn't understand how eM could stay in that position and continue to write for hours on end, and rock to the same beat...and on occasion, there were a few words he would utter...

"Ay yo, start that shit over" or even "Turn that up for me thunthun..."

...and after he sat and wrote for three hours, eM realized he had to go back to the hood and handle the business he was trying to avoid for mad long..."...maybe today it won't be like that..." eM thought as he went to the soundboard and turned the master volume down to a tone where he could actually hear his thoughts...

The door opened..."you gon' go deaf one day wit this shit that loud Emil..." That was his producer's cue...anytime there was a level decrease, he knew a phase of Emil's development had ended..."...You heard me eM...?"

Emil looked back at his producer with the grin he always let out when he was sick of being advised on his life 'cause he had decided he was gonna do it his way anyway...

"Hehheh...I know...but once I put my album out, then I can slow down and think...but I gotta go hard right now, word..." he closed his composition book and began to pack his fake Jansport knapsack...

"You outta here...?"

"Yeah, I'm a ghost...I gotta get back to the hood and handle some b.i., bee..."

"Yo, you need some cheddar sun, 'cause if you do I got'chu..."

"Nah man, you know how I feel about tak—"

Before eM could even finish, his man cut him right off..."NAH MAN, *YOU* know how I feel about you goin' out there on that dummy shit sun...don't tell me you fuckin' wit them nigguhs now, sun...that's how you gittin' down now...?"

Emil shook his head and let out a sigh..."Nah man, I'm not rockin' wit them kats, but I gotta go and check PM real fast and see what the haps is..."

His producer gave him the icy stare that froze his whole train of thought now 'cause he was younger...he would later give that same grill back on the world, perfected...eM would teach them how to rock it...right now though, he was rocked by it...

"You need to stop ac'in stupid Emil...you got a future right here in this...it don't matter how you git to the top...just don't blow it all away...if you do it right now, you will make it, but you gotta have faith in yourself sun..."

"Come on now...you know I'm the illest rhyme writer alive thunthun...the only dude spittin' that got some shit on me is G Rap sun...otha' than that, these kats need to make way...just wait sun..."

"Aight" his producer said... "Just don't get caught up in they negativity...it will leave you locked up or dead...just keep goin' hard sun...look at how your brother does it sun...the way he does it in school is the way you need to do it with these rhymes if you gon' make it up outta here sun...remember, he made it out...now it's your turn..."

"Yeah, I know..." Emil felt conflicted about that topic...eM and his brother were the two smartest outta the four of them...Christian had made a ill power move, getting a full scholarship to the prep school outta state...shit, they even paid for him to go there, eM thought, referring to Christian's stipend that allowed him to bring home the illest champion sweatshirts for free, the ones that were especially made for his school, with logos and numbers that couldn't be found on the ones from Modell's... "he made a ill move ...I'ma do the same shit though...wit this rap game sun...watch..."

His producer, now receiving the look he had just given, quivered for a second from eM's tenacity and spirit that were overwhelming...he knew Emil would do it all... "aight yo, that's what I'm talkin' about, just don't get caught up...go to the crib and leave PM and them nigguhs alone, aight...now what up, you sure you don't need that dough...?..."

And eM didn't know if he would need it or not, but eM knew he might once he got home to assess the damage alchemy caused in his chasm called apartment 4A... "nah, I'ma be aight...good lookin' though..." He picked up his certy, mad at the fact that even his producer knew how drastic it was...but eM never let anyone onto his pain, instead it only fueled the fire that burned inside for this game to come to him...and it was only a matter of time...it was not now though...eM went to his man, gave him a pound in the form of a stiff hood handshake...his producer put his free arm around eM in an embrace similar to half a hug and got in his ear whispering the words "be safe out there thun...we need you here..."

"You know me..." was eM's reply...

"EXACTLY...that's why I said it..."

"Don't wet it yo…I'm outta here…peace…"

"Later yo…"

As one hand went right into Emil's pocket, the other hand lifted, leaving two fingers in the form of his words, his favorite symbol of hood sign language that spoke louder than his words and rang harder than his rhymes…'cause he was a peaceful kat…but for every side, there was another…Emil took the stairs down, sick of his producer's pissy elevator…busting out on the ground floor, he exited the building and walked right into what seemed to be the routine stickup…to his left in front of the adjacent building, three kids encircled a newcomer like vultures swooping in on the dead, like a lioness engulfing a gazelle that wasn't quick enough to hop past her quick claws…newcomers knew not to come to this hood…Emil caught a little pc based on the fact he was always checkin' his producer…besides that, them street-corner kats knew not to test his gangster…because the ones that let eM's five-foot-two frame fool them got lumped up and stomped out by the chaos unleashed from his little body in the form of unstoppable rage that even five kats couldn't contain…as the building door closed shut, the newcomer looked in eM's direction, hoping his presence might stop the violent venom of the snake-like scavengers which encircled him…and as the carcass looked his last view of life, one of the vultures swiftly outstretched his neck and head, swirling toward eM and giving the look of death, as if eye to eye with the grim reaper…and that expression exhausted itself with the knowledge of the recipient…

"What up eM…you fuckin' wit this right here bee…?" one of the vultures squawked…the mark hoped that eM words might save him from the inevitable instance of the stickup he had just walked into...

"Nah, I'm cool thunthun...I'm on the move...y'all do what'chu gotta do, I'ma catch you on a later note..."

"Aight yo, be safe..." the vulture replied...the remark the mark knew he hadn't comprehended, given the circumstances...

Emil pulled the black hood over his head as if mourning the site of death...and as he walked and turned to the right, he gave his usual sign of superiority that kept him out of the hood drama... "Peace cousin" eM replied as he turned from their sight and kept it moving to the train station...and just before he turned, he looked in the face of the mark who was shook, scared to death and scared to look...his fear pierced Emil's conscience...for never did eM think he would be involved in such a chaotic cycle...he looked back at the carcass, piercing his soul with eyes that asked him one question before eM bounced..."if you a out-a-towner, what the fuck you doin' floatin' through this crazy-ass hood...?...for that violation, you get what'cha deserve..." eM didn't get a chance to see the reply, for as he began to turn back to his own plans, he could see out the corner of his eye as the vultures surrounded him and began to eat in a cycle created by Darwinian Hoodonomics—SURVIVal of thE fiTtEST...eM he saw the mark fall from grace as he was eaten and swallowed in a surreal function of reality he didn't think, for some reason, was true of this hood... "I bet'cha that nigguh'll know the next fuckin' time..."

And with the same swiftness he used in leaving his hood, eM hopped up the stairs to the elevated set of turnstiles, hopped over the three-pronged metal divider, and hopped onto the next train before the token booth operator could even respond "Hey, stop," or before the cops could catch him for his small-time-petty-crime...as the subway train bell tolled twice announcing its departure, Emil slid through the crack in the doors just as they began to close...as the train slowly pulled off from the platform, he could see the two cops chasing the train to catch him, but too slow to react based on the Dunkin' Donuts stop five minutes before he had arrived...Emil looked at them through the plexiglass windows on the doors...and he gave his usual grin, knowing he caught a W while these stupid-slow-ass-cops caught a L from the swift little thun...some of the people in the train car shook they heads, while he laughed out loud at the pigs...and as po-Lice followed the train that began to speed up, he gave three signs with only two hands...digging into his left jacket pocket, he pulled out his school train pass and put it to the window...and he couldn't stop laughing...then, with his right hand, he used only one limb...eM stuck'em with the solitary disrespect of one digit, his middle finger...finally, as the train sped off into the darkness of the tunnel he had been notorious for taggin' up in, he put the train pass back in his pocket and came out with the norm, two fingers...

"Peace PoPo..."

And all the people who had given him that look of disappointment at his derelict deeds sharply turned away, once his eyes surveyed the entire car of the train in one glance...

"WHUUUT!! I got a train pass...who got beef...?"

The only response came from silence, which usually

didn't have any sort of conflict with him being right, whether correct or mistaken...eM turned left and looked at the two-seater at the end of the car...there was one kat sitting there already, but as he realized eM was on his way in that direction, he sorely submitted and got up to squeeze in between the two people in the three-seater, who were heated as what little space they did have, evaporated...without a word, thun sat in the red-carpeted seat left for him...he slouched in, nestled his hoodie to the side of his face, and opened the door to slumber as he let the enterprise float him back to what seemed like the other side of the world — the galaxy of Queens...

Emil began walking back through his block, and upon entering the opening that exposed the basketball courts, he saw his whole clique on the benches interacting in the everyday modus operandi of smoking blunts and passing a few forties...

"Ay yo, there go eM...thuuuuuuuuuuuuuuuun..." Eddy was the one with the razor-sharp-vision like the OG g.o.d.father that knew and saw all, whether there or not...

"Yeahyeah...what up y'all..." Emil replied and circling the cypher, gave pounds, hugs and love to each and every one of his peoples...and after he touched base with his last mans, he went right to Eddy... "Let me hit that sunthun," and before Eddy could get his puff of smoke, swift-ass eM's swift hands had taken the blunt right outta E's mouth, put it in his, pulled twice, and blew the smoke in his face...the whole crew starting laughing as if Eddie Murphy had done a live performance of Raw right there on top of the backboard…eM was a funny dude like that…

"You a funny dude sunsun, word up…" were the only words as half his clique laughed, and a few spit out the poison, choking from the comedy eM always displayed…

"Little fast-ass muthafucka" Eddy mumbled under his breath right in eM face…but it was only seconds before he started to let out a chuckle himself, knowing he just had gotten got for his trees…"…where you comin' from sun…?"

"Writing in the studio, you know my style…I got some new shit fo' dat' ass yo, word…who wanna battle…"

And like the train, only silence responded…his whole clique looked to him as a visionary, secretly writing rhymes with the hopes that he would blow and take them with him…eM took another few pulls of smoke off the El, only to hear E yelling "Aight sun, it's bad enough you got me, don't smoke my whole shit sun…" Melquan passed Eddy the forty, and no sooner than he touched it had Emil took his last puff of weed smoke, snatched the forty, put the El in the hand that E once used to hold the bottle, turned it up to his mouth, and swigged until it was almost gone…

J'on looked right at Eddy and yelled "Damn E, for a nigguh that see everything, why you never see eM comin' sun…?" Everybody laughed again as eM deaded what was left of the forty leaving just enough to take it away from his mouth and pour the remainder on the floor, a usual ritual for his hood, pouring liquor out for all his peoples who hadn't made it in life long enough to be there with them on this cold winter day…

"DAMN THUN...YOU KNOW I ALWAYS POUR LIQUOR OUT BEFORE I DRINK...YOU JUST DEADED SOME GOOD ASS ST. IDES!!!"

"You ain't need it" was eM's reply, and softly chuckling he said, "You know you my man though...where PM at thunthun...?"

His whole crew's expressions changed, and shifting humor to somber, they looked at him knowing what he was getting at...

"He on the block sun...he was over here lookin' for you...you movin' wit thun now...?"
"Nah, I just gotta talk wit'em about some shit...yo, you shoulda seen this cornball I seen getting robbed today sun...shook-ass-nigguh in the wrong hood at the wrong time..."
"VUL-TURES" Earl said, who always spoke in one-word sentences that summed up the story short before it became long...
"No doubt sun...yo, who upstairs...?"
"Deem up there, and your sister..." one of the Twins tolled out..."...we was just up there a minute ago," said Twin number two, who usually had to finish or had his sentences finished by his kin who came right before him...
"Aight, I'ma git up wit' y'all in a minute..." Emil said as he left the cypher to go upstairs...
"Oh, E..." and as his words were hittin' his man's eardrums to be processed, eM had already snatched the

blunt a second time, turned around and bounced sayin'
"Yo, Deem need to hit this, I'll be back…"…he could hear
his crew's laughter in the background decrease in volume
as he floated to the building door, up the stairs and
unlocked the door, into apartment 4A…

Deem was sitting in the window, looking out onto the
world as he always did through the cold steel window
bars that trapped his mental in a way none would know
for years…

"What up D…want this shit…?" as eM finished taking
his last pull, and passed it to Deem…"…Nah man, fuck
dat, I ain't smokin', ain't no food in the crib man, I'm
fuckin' starving…give me some money sun…" was
Deem's response…

"Didn't Mommy get the check today?" Emil asked his
brother with a tone in his voice that normally preceded his
sporadic spazz-out sessions…

"Yeah she got that shit…go see E for it…you know
how that go…she in the back laid the fuck out…" Emil
hated this, 'cause it was this adult behavior that made him
head right over to PM's block and be an adult ahead of his
time… "Damn…" eM whispered to himself as he put the
El down in the ashtray on the table and slid through the
living room to the cracked bedroom doorway of his
cracked-out mom…eM looked and saw her sprawled out
across the bed, hovering in a ubiquitous euphoria that he
could not understand…

"Mommy" he said softly but firmly… "There's no food
in the house, can I get some money to get some food…"

68

Silence was the reply..."MOMMY" he shouted this time...

"WHAT THE FUCK YOU YELLIN' AT ME FOR..." was the violent response of his mother, who had just been brought back to earth because of his shattering presence in her cracked-out essence...

"Mommy, there's no food..."

"I know, go get some..."

"Can I have some money please...?"

"I don't got it...go next door and ask Ms. Joann if you can borrow five dollars and go to the supermarket..."

"Yeah...aight..." eM didn't even argue with her, he knew it wasn't even worth it...he closed her door, and as he walked out to the living room, his little sister Akilah came out of her room, hearing his voice... "eM, can I have a dollar to go get some food..."

"I'm goin' to the store right now, I'll be back..." eM replied to her...he picked up the El from the ashtray to finish it himself...he would need to have the weed in him to forget about what he had to do... "Where you goin' sun?" Deem asked...

"I'ma go check PM real fast sunsun...I'll be back in a minute...watch Kila, Mommy too fucked up to know anything..."

"Why you think I'm up here...?...Hurry up sun, I wanna go outside..."

"Aight" Emil replied, walking out the door, skipping down eight small broken flights, out his building and back to the cypher...he took one last pull and passed the El

69

right back to Eddy… "Oh, good lookin' out" E responded… "I told you you my man, right?" questioned Emil, and just as fast as he had took it, he was out, two blocks across and one over to link up with PM…

"WHO YOU WIT' NIGGUH…" PM's greeting to all that came across his path…right now, it was for Emil, who was on his way upstairs to the apartment via PM throwing the door keys out the window because the intercom stayed broke, buzzing no one in…

"GAHT DAMN EMIL, HOW MANY TIMES I GOTTA TELL YOU SUN…" was PM's response right before eM had cut him off…

"I know sun, but—"

"BUT NUFIN YO! You gotta think about this shit for real, sun…it's real out here, you don't need to be doin' what we doin', you got a future sun…this is a dead-end life with a dead-end death…"…PM was one of the realest gangsters in the hood…as a matter of fact, he might have even been the realest before other kats came up…and it wasn't that he was a menace…his was average: average height, average weight, and he even looked average with the bald-head-Kojak-ed-mecca that everyone in the hood rocked…but that was what made him who he was, because PM was so regular, he just blended in unnoticed, completely anonymous…a good quality to have when one let the gun bust as much as PM made bullets spin into other kats he was at war with for whatever reason…

"You know I know how real it is…man, my little sister can't even eat yo, you know my moms ain't right right

70

now…" Emil had to look down to the floor, because he was ashamed he had to describe the situation in this way…"…if there's anyone who knows how fuckin' real it is, it's me sun, you know that…"

"You need to tell your mans-n-them to stop pumpin' that shit to her, that's against the code thunthun…"…PM replied…"I ain't gonna be that dude sun, you know that's against the code, too…" cM was a kat full of integrity, following all the codes of the streets and especially adhering to the codes of the hood he ran in…

"Yeah, you right…" and that's what PM liked about him, PM knew he was real smart and had a lot of potential in the rap game if he stayed focused on his plan…but until he got his record deal, PM knew how serious it was for eM…

"C'mon Paul, you my last hope right now sun…you know I got'chu as soon as I get on…but until then sun, I need you to look out for me…what it look like sun…?" PM knew he had to listen when eM began to call him by his government…

PM, which stood for Paul Michael, Power and Money, and Pussy Man every once in awhile, sat in the chair and let out a deep sigh as his small hands ran across the span of his bald head…and he didn't want to make it what it was turning into, but he knew if eM was gonna do it, he'd rather have his little-ass on his side than on the opposing…he loved eM like a little brother, every time PM saw him, it was like looking in the mirror and reminiscing on his younger self…as if they were one in the same…

"Aight sun...I'll let you rock with me...here's how it's gonna go down..."

eM's spirits lifted, knowing his ghetto architecture was beginning to build a construct he despised, but had to work in until he could do it the right way...

"Pay attention sun...there's this cornball that my little sister fuckin' with...he a real sheisty character sun, 'cause he only come around when he know I'm out on the block working...on the phone and all that he play bitch, but my peoples been tellin' me about how he shittin' on me and my gangster...so here's the drill...you wanna be down wit me sun...?" PM already knew what the answer would be, but he had to give Emil the chance to accept or refuse this mission... "Don't ask me no stupid questions!!!" responded eM...

"Aight then..." he went into the back room for a few seconds and when he reemerged, he held two shiny gats..."...You wanna shine like chrome or rock wit black steel in the hour of chaos..."...eM's eyes opened wide and with the animal instinct that overtook him, he reached for the black gat quick...the shiny black nine fit in eM's hand as if it were destined to be there...

"Yeah...that's my favorite shit too...now here's the drilly...I want you to lay up for him...once I bounce, it'll probably only be a hour or two before this nigguh show up...he a light-skinned kat, he look pretty regular...but you'll know him by his fuckin' jewels...I want you to stick him..."

"I don't gotta kill thun right," was Emil's first response, concerned with the fact that he didn't want to take a life...PM smirked, knowing eM would only buck under kill or be killed circumstances...that's why he was gonna eM him rock with his favorite heat, 'cause he knew it would come back to him clean, just as clean as it was when it left... "Nah man, just stick him...bring me back the jewels...you do that, I'll hit you wit some paper for the jewels, and put you down sun...how dat sound...?"

"Like music to my ears..." eM quickly cocked the top back, and held it to make sure the bullet was in the chamber, released the safety and began to aim around PM crib...

"YO, STOP PLAYIN' WIT THAT SHIT SUN...USE THAT SHIT!!!"

"WHAT THE FUCK, YOU THINK I'M NOT NIGGUH?!?!" eM replied with a serious nature in his tone...this was for his family to eat...he could starve, but his sister was too little not to have no food...and with what the hood had done...eM lowered the gat and put the safety on... "Call me in my crib when you about to skate, and I'll come back on the late night creep..." eM instructed PM..."Now remember," PM explained, "no bodies, not even blood...JUST THE JEWELS, aight?" eM stopped looking lustfully at the gat and as he moved his eyes back into the zone of PM's he replied, "No doubt sun, I got this...just have that paper ready for me..." PM trusted eM beyond belief, and even though he wasn't down with PM and his clique, he trusted eM more than he trusted most kats in his crew that he did his worse dirt with...he dug into his pocket and pulled out a heavy green fold of mixed money...it was all dirty though..."Here thun," PM said,

73

peeling off five twenties for eM's empty pockets... "Go git your sister some food and I'll hit you in the crib when I'm outta here..."

This was the moment of truth, and eM didn't know what to do...PM could see the apprehension in his character and said "what, you don't want it...?...ain't this shit what you came for muthafucka...?...you better take this dough before the next man do..." eM looked back down at the gat, then across at the yard waiting for him...and he took the money, knowing he had a new topic for his next story-rhyme... "I know I don't gotta tell you, but I gotta tell you...don't front on me sun, you know how I feel about that...and you know what that will mean..." And even though PM's words held no personal weight, he had to say them for they would hold weight in the way eM moved...and eM knew how real these words were... "No doubt sun...you know I'm not the type to front...don't even try to play me like that..." and with that, eM gave PM a pound and a hug, stashed the gat in his waist underneath the certy jacket, went to the door and on his way out shouted his essence that was soon to be conflicted dichotomously... "Peace Paul..." giving him the two fingers that would soon be the ones to squeeze for him...

"I'll be on the block sun, just come find me after you regulate that fool..."

Emil skated to the Chinese food restaurant, threw a twenty through the bulletproof partition, and in exchange received 4 chicken wings with fries for his sister, a cheeseburger with fries for his brother, and General Tso's chicken with fried rice for himself...he thought about his mom but reality set in for him... "she'll be too high to eat anyway..." He grabbed the bag and skated back to 4A...

He came through the door to his sister and brother waiting like craving crackheads who had sent the messenger on a re-up run, to obtain hit number two...they were starving, and eM knew he could not let them down...he gave his sister her food and sent her to her room to eat so he could talk to Deem and save her virgin ears from the scathe and scourge of the hood life they lived...

"Yo, let me come wit you sun, you gonna need me..." Deem told him...

"HELL NO!!!...I don't need you, sun...it's gotta be clean..." eM told him, knowing that bringing his brother was worse than bringing the grim reaper himself...because eM, he'd just stick'em...but Deem, he'd be more concerned with catchin' a body, *and that,* even The Father of the Badlands Mob couldn't afford to pay for... "I'm good sun...here man, hurry up and go get some weed and come right back to the house so I can handle this b.i. sun..." eM's words to Deem as he slid him the second twenty... "DAMN SUN! He hit you already?...you sure you don't—"

"NO" eM said, cutting into Deem's response before he even finished... "Ga'head before I gotta bounce sun..." Deem took the twenty and asking no questions, shook his head, grabbed Emil's coat, and with motion in exact

75

opposition to his brother, slowly slid through the crib and out the door...eM went into his room and switched up clothes, straight black apparel, his creepin' uniform...after he changed, he sat on the bed with the door closed and began to stare at the gat...eM knew there was no turning back from here...an hour later, the phone rang and the locks to the door began to click simultaneously...

"Yo..." answered eM as he picked up the phone...

"Meet me in the park in front of my building in like ten minutes..." PM mused through the phone... "I'm there in five" eM responded, as he now saw Deem coming through the door...eM hung up the phone, looked at his brother who moved in slow motion and his only words were "You always did have good timing...Peace..."

"Be safe out there, and call me if you get into some shit..." eM knew he would not call Deem because he wasn't gonna git in no shit...this was a straight stick-and-move, and that's what he'd do, stick and move...

"Gimme my certy sun..." the words as eM snatched the coat he and Deem shared because Deem's coat money got smoked last week...

eM laid up in the building staircase like he was waiting on money...nose runny and brain flooded in the cold-ass corridor, he stood in between the stairs that separated floor six and the roof...and from the window, he looked upon the world like the owl, eyes wide open, omniscient and ready to do what he needed to do...

And now the time had come...perched on his tippytoes peering out the window, eM could see the high yellow

76

complexion of a kat whose face was unrecognizable from almost seven stories high...but he could see the sky-blue-grade of the ice glistening underneath the light of the awning that covered every single building in his projects...eM now concentrated on his hearing, pushing all else outta his head so he could hear the door... "cLIckKLUng"...and he could hear the mark ascending towards his downward spiral...eM knew footsteps in the project hallways all too well...and as soon as he could no longer hear the ascent, eM knew that he was on that landing...he darted down the stairs, pulling the gat from out of his waist and releasing the safety to red which in the hood meant ready to rock...and as the mark made it to floor two, eM was already down near floor four and for the mark, their coincidental collision would transpire on the platform of floor three...eM pulled the ski mask over the bottom of his face, covering all from the nose down...and with his hoodie and skullie cap covering his head, all that remained was his eyes...and as the mark turned on the landing, he was met at the stairs by a gat dead in his throat...

"Give it up fast, you know the drill..." eM uttered... and with that he paused...he knew there was something about the jewels that looked all too familiar, even from his perch on high...his eyes piercing the face of the mark who didn't know whether to back down or back this nigguh in his way down...and here lie the rub...face to face, eye to eye, Emil had been placed in a dichotomous dilemma...for he had the cold black steel aimed, pushed right into the larynx of the mark...

He wished he would've known this was the mark...eM looked in Eddy's face and tried to conceal his knowledge of the situation...and whether Paul Michael had set him up or not, it was going down now...and he could choose to either take his architecture skills to *build* with his newfound-fam'ly in *destroying* his man, or build with his man in destroying a plot he had already agreed to and been paid for...

And Emil knew it was not the way...his path let him know the Word said not to steal...his thoughts, frantic in his cranium, kept him on edge... "If I don't do this, my little sister can't eat...me and my brother can starve all day, but not Akilah..."...and the gat quivered in his hand, and it was undistinguishable as to whether it was his hand holding the gat or if it were the larynx of Eddy, who wasn't pussy, and normally would not back down...

"You take these jewels and you don't leave *this* hood alive my nigguh...these right here is *my* projects...you won't make it out alive..."...were the only words Eddy could utter, knowing he couldn't even make a move to his gat 'cause right now, he had gotten got again...only Eddy didn't know it was the kat that stayed gittin' him on the regular...

Emil pulled the hammer back, letting Eddy know it was no game..."Just come up outta that shit quick homie...right now...or get the pound..." and here he was, face to face with a violation that he would not be able to reconcile or even explain...because now it was too late...

...and here was eM's torture...

But it had already begun...now it had to go down...

7—Thou shalt not commit adultery.

The Holy Bible, King James Version, Exodus 20:14

7—God (Allah)

Supreme Mathematics

...choose which one to use...

"**W**HY THE FUCK THIS NIGGUH CALLIN' YOU...?...HE KNOW I WAS OUTTA TOWN..."

"WELL, WHY DON'T YOU ASK HIM...THAT'S *YOUR* MAN!!!"

"NAH, FUCK THAT...YOU THE ONE HERE WIT ME...WHY HE CALLIN' FOR YOU...?"

Christian was yelling at Ayesha for no apparent reason...and he knew in his heart she was right, he needed to check his man for trying to play what seemed to be some slick shit...Christian was trying to build a foundation with her, his man's name was not to be involved in any of that... Chris was trying to take her to the top...this kat, however, would stay where he was when they departed...but there was something about it, for between his own guilt with his wandering eyes that never strayed and uncontrollable urges of pathetic polygamy, Christian's confusion came from his own chest cavity...maybe if he were able to talk to Ayesha about it, things would be better...that's how it was supposed to work...however, he was scared, too scared to lose her 'cause he thought she wouldn't be able to understand those conversations...they were in a rut worse than world wars waged on the trade...and instead of trying to really figure it out, there were just times that he would argue *at* her in his own mental frustration with himself...

"You fuckin' wit this dude...?...why you fuckin' wit this nigguh...?" Christian asked knowing in his heart of hearts the last thought on Ayesha's mind was this cornball kat...or maybe it wasn't...

"You think I'm fuckin' wit him...you want me to tell you I'm fuckin' him...you know I wouldn't lie to you...so I don't know what to tell you..."

This response from Ayesha enraged him even more, because the truth hurt...and the fact of the matter was she was right, he knew she wasn't even thinking about this character...but the chaos in his environment had quickly become the chaos in his mind, overflooding his sense of rationale to a point where anything was possible...and even though he analyzed every angle, now his analysis was thwarted to a point that was detrimental to his entire person...he had lost himself somewhere along the line...and he tried to trap himself because ultimately, the torture of the truth hurt...he knew all she wanted was him...and her life was now what he wanted it to be because as he was doing things, she as well tried to deal with eradicating the inconsequential to make him happy...and now, here he was, not believing the one person in which he could have faith...

"FUCK THAT...I CAN'T BELIEVE YOU FUCKIN' WIT THIS NIGGUH...I DO EVERYTHING FOR YOU... AND NOW YOU FUCKIN' AROUND WIT THIS KAT..."

"...Whatever Christian..." she uttered, her tone exhaling exhaustion...their fights were becoming entirely too much, because she knew, and she knew he knew...and he did...however, he had only known one way, the one taught to him previous...so he worked in that realm now...and it was too bad, because they loved each other...there had been no love prior to her...it was just that Chris hadn't learned or didn't know how to do it...and with that, he didn't do the smart thing—follow her example—but instead borrowed the blueprint of preceding paths...when would he realize that portal had led him to his dearest Ayesha...?

"Where are you going...?" she said in a soft voice that struggled to restrain her bubbling tears because she didn't want him to go...she wished they could talk and work through their turmoil...she knew she was just as unsuccessful as he, and there were things that if she told him now, he wouldn't be able to understand...neither of them knew where they were or where it had gone...but it wasn't what it was supposed to be...regardless, she couldn't bear it again, for she hated it when he left...Ayesha was just as headstrong as Christian, so she wouldn't back down when it was on...and if she didn't back down, thun would keep going, but he loved her just because she was that strong and wouldn't back down...even he did not know where it went, but he was just as scared as she...

"I'ma just go and take a drive...I gotta clear my head..." Christian was mad yet at the same time, he had to do something drastic to make the situation either come to a head in conflict, or go away once he got back from driving around thinkin' about...

"...please don't leave..."

"...I can't take it...I'll be back..."

"...alright..."

They continued to break each other's hearts in their downward spiral...in the meantime, Christian grabbed his new-navy-blue-Yankee in a hurry, pulling it down and to the side, covering the upper flap of his left ear, leaving much of the right side of his head exposed to the outer world...he looked in her eyes and could see the torture that was a reflection of his reciprocated back to her...she saw similar to him...and he could only look in her eyes for an interval similar to lightspeed...he quickly turned from the coat rack on the wall, walked past her a few steps and grabbing his keys on the way down the hallway to the back of the crib, floated with land's speed to the back door...he didn't even lock it anymore..."if she wants to be safe, she'll git up and lock it..." he thought to himself, confused in his action, for it was not him...he knew not what had taken him, but if there was one thing Chris did know, this was not him...he didn't know where he was or how he went...but he did know how to unlock the door to his whip, swiftly plopping in the plush leather seat that encapsulated his essence as if the company had tailor-made it to his physical specifics...he jammed the key in the ignition and before the engine could ignite, he had already slammed the trannie into drive, and burning rubber, murked off out the driveway, to the left, past the stop sign and off into the darkness of street life...

Christian didn't know what was goin' on, but he knew that just maybe, if he drove long enough, all of these newfound issues would miraculously disappear into thin air...he drove straight and started to ease his emotions as his personal envoy floated him further away from where he was supposed to be...grabbing the brim of his hat as he always had, he handled his usual routine of relieving stress by creating friction as he tilted the brim on his head back and forth, causing the binding of the fitted cap to rub against his head hard enough to emit the dandruff of his dry scalp...the 360 degrees of waves that splashed around his head like the ocean had subsided, leaving only trace marks of fluid...now, it was a barren wasteland...

"...fuck, I can't take this shit..." he said out loud, talking to his car who always listened...if only he could hear the advice it gave...dipping through stop signs and green lights, he wound up on that other side of town...this was where he copped his dirt chronic..."...the pillow factory..." he thought, which was notorious for pumpin' them fat two-El nicks that he could split even further...he loved to burn it with Ayesha...now, he didn't know what was going on...

Christian made his usual stop at the late-night-convenient-spot and copped a twenty-two of St. Ide's at his earliest convenience, which this time, was later than early but morning for his bloodlines, the nighttime vultures... "the danney will git my mind off this shit..." he said aloud to himself as the Arab at the register looked at him as if he were losing hold of his mind that had already escaped him...and Christian knew he had to give this up along with his many worldly vices that propelled him deeper into a vortex of the void that increased as his undying love for Ayesha decreased with every argument, every unresolved issue ...he grabbed the bottle bound in the brown paper bag and before entering the running car, cracked the top, spilled out the first three swigs and shouted "What the fuck is this about Deem...?"

Too bad thun didn't answer his questions when they had to be rectified in the worldly...Deem was elsewhere...

Shooting swigs of sour fluid through his throat into his stomach, he hoped it would flow to his bloodstream and into his brain as soon as possible...this drink, he thought, would in fact drown the pain and the sorrow he could not come to terms with...as he drove and drank, he passed past the pottery plant again, and could see to his left out the corner of his eye a shorty standing on the corner, waving in his direction to drive over...and since his mind was not warding off its chaos, the envious environment ensued, taking him down a road he knew he was not to tread...he had made too many promises, he had called in too many favors and convened with too many spirits to now take it here...but he didn't know what to do...

He made a left turn right past shorty, and as the oncoming traffic ceased, proceeded to make a u-turn back past her again...and even while the Great Word told him to pass before committing this vehement violation of the seventh carved sentence on the second of two tablets, he stopped, pulling over for this woman...he hit the computerized control on the door, which enabled the window to fall in the same way he would...

"Can I ride wit'chu...?"

"Yeah, c'mon..." Chris said as he used the power to unlock the door and resurrect the window from its ground level...she got in the car and sat down...

"...This is a nice car...it fits you, like they built it just fa' your fly-ass..." she said in an effort to spark some conversation and stroke his ego...

"...thanks..." was Christian's reply, not really knowing how to take it, because he hadn't been in this type of situation with a woman for awhile, and definitely wasn't supposed to be now that he had her there...

"What's your name?" she asked him...

"...Mike..." knowing full well his lies would lure him further into the trap he had tripped himself up in...

"...what about you, ma...?"

"...Out here on the streets, they call me Coko..." Christian could see how her dark-chocolate complexion coerced the hood into that moniker...however, it was his bewilderment with her wonder that would leave him locked down in a snare...he was analyzing the bait, but the question was, would temptation tempt him enough, wrapping him like the silly rabbit lunging for the carrot in between the sharp metal teeth that bit worse than they barked once the weight of the orange stick triggered the teeth's taste for blood...he continued to swallow heavily while seeing through newly-slanted eyelids as shorty said "I'cah see you been through some shit...all this dough you paid on this whip, and you still drinkin' malt liquor..."

"...that's the hood in me, love...you wouldn't understand that..."

"…look at where I'm at nigguh…I understand more than you know, wit'cha cute-ass…"
…and he knew if she were out here working like this, that shit was real…but for some reason, he felt in his youthish wisdom, that no one knew his pain…yet he still could not recognize it was only emotion, nothing more…and nothing less…she took her index finger and ran the back of it across his right cheek which quivered with her touch to let her know this was not his usual procedure in the slightest…"…I don't bite…unless you want me to…"
"…I don't really git down like this…"
"…as if I didn't know that already…" she read his mind which moved monotonously mundane to her yet lighter than speed to him… "yeah, I guess you would…" he said softly, scared of where he had been led…and in his hysteria, he only had himself to blame for choosing to move left as opposed to right at this juncture called disjunction, forked at a road rearing a righteous and a wicked path…and in a split second of remorse, he stopped walking…
"…listen…" said Christian…"I think that I shou—"
"I can tell you in some shit, whatever it may be…" Coko chanted before he could even turn back and choose a different decision deemed destiny… "I don't really know, but what I do know is that I'ma 'bout to take you and suck ya' sexy ass off…"
..with her left hand, she began to slowly rub his right thigh…and she was surprised to see his erection had not unfolded…"that'll change in a minute, don't wet dat…go

down that way…I'ma show you why they call me Chocolate-Wondah…"

Christian was now fearful of the sin that seemingly suppressed him…"look, I don't have no dough, so I think it's best that I just drop you off…"

"…this one's on me cutie…"

"…LOOK, I AIN'T TRYIN' TO FUCK…"

"…and what makes you think I'ma give this good pussy to you in the first place…?…you can't afford that…but I will suck you off better than any bitch you've ever known in yo' life…and the next time you get some dough, believe me you gonna bring it ova' here to this side…"

He couldn't control the emerging urgency of his second brain…it had taken control of him like it did for almost every man…he was tryin' to be different…but he could feel the blood rushing from one head to another…he turned back around and started walking down the path he had stopped traveling on…

They drove down the deserted block…she instructed him to round the next two blocks and then pull over…and as he was doing that, she questioned him only once…as he proceeded to park with one hand, he used the other to go into his wallet and pull out a green-faced dime…

"…keep it…" Coko said… "I love dark chocolate…this one's on me…"

Christian turned the ignition off, deaded the lights and could feel her unzipping the fly of his jeans and reaching into the opening left…

"…DAMN…" she said, "…I knew it…y'all dark skinny brothas always got it…"

...and with that, she turned in the seat, bent at her back, and plunged him into her mouth slowly, moving until she had consumed him...and with this hood life and it's chaos which his brain was dead to, his other half was alive and kicking...he felt conflicted, knowing he didn't want her to do it...but in an instant, he understood the wonder of her ways...his dome dropped back on the headrest and his eyes slowly closed...and all he could see was Ayesha...he wished he weren't here, but his counterpart rationalized quickly for him...for Ayesha, while she loved him with all she had, was not a fan of delivering headspins...so he let Coko whine up and down, consuming all he had to offer...and there was a lot to work with...and she was working it with all she had...and somewhere along the way, Christian lost sight of the *God* he was working with...this was another one of the worldly vices he had to conquer victoriously...

...unfortunately, he was losing here...
For while he loved Ayesha, his texture was tormented through tangible tales and melodic memories in the form of flashbacks that fueled his sexual exploits...and his lack of communication courted his feelings of inadequacy, making him kneel not before the God he revered, but instead towards his nymphonic notions, erotic exploits and pornographic phases which led him to the dark sinful side of his perplexed psyche...he hadn't conquered it and so his sex addiction made him think he needed that...it would only be later that Christian would find this adulterous act and life fable a fictitious falsity...

And he tried to fight the feeling, but between the St.
Ide's and the tobacco he was slowly pulling on, he entered
this deceitful dungeon...and now holdin' the back of her
head, his hand hovered up and down with her movements
and he let out a sigh of relief, relishing...rendered by her
forceful foulness in what she thought was her right to
do...and as she mumbled he moaned through her slurps
and swallows...

"...I am so...

...sorry...

...Ay...es..."

And as she had brought him to the point of no return, he
felt the rush of his head filling, and as the determined dam
was about to break and overflow...

.........BBBBBBBEEEEEEEEEEEEEEEEPPPPPPPPPP.........

Christian awoke to the blaring horn, in the car
alone...he looked around and, as the gas had almost
exhausted itself from the tank, realized he had not even
pulled off from the driveway...there were no signs of
empty bottles marking the end of any danney...he took his
hand off the horn, and as he looked down, he realized his
mind had been playing tricks on him the way Houston had
given rise to the Geto Boyz in the eighties...there was,
however, one sign of his mental mistake...he wiped his

face, trying to clear the cold from sleep caught in the corners of his eyes...and as he turned off the car, he went to wipe the ashes off his lap from the tobacco which had burned all the way through to the end...and as he pulled one end of his pants to flick the ashes up in the air so as not to smear his apparel, he realized it was too late...he was submerged in a sloppy puddle of his own semen...

"Git the fuck outta here..." Christian exclaimed, as he realized this entire episode was merely a dream...and quite a wet one at that...

...yet the remains were all too real...

"SHIT..." he thought, wondering how he was to get back in the house without being caught for an act that only his second head and lustful imagination had committed...

He got up and stepping out the car, locked the doors after sticking the Club to the wheel...and when he saw the security light blinking to confirm the activation of the car alarm, he began to wake up and quickly think "How am I gonna get back in the house..."...first he thought he could make it through the basement back door...but busting through that way would only cause more commotion as he realized the two-by-four was blocking not only his entrance, but any intruder's who thought shit was sweet ...to walk around to the front of the house would definitely bring Ayesha out of any slumber he hoped she was in, for of the three doors that needed to be entered, the noise of one of them would certainly trigger her bionic ears to his return...he was left with only the kitchen, climbing the stairs which led to the back door...

He snuck through slowly to be greeted by his cat, who he quickly picked up before she screamed her sacred meows that preceded his presence...he stroked her head a few times and then lightly dropped her to the floor...and as his pet ran through the house down to the basement, even she looked at him with shame and disgust...if the cat can't understand, what woman on earth would...?

Christian quietly began to disrobe as he tip-toed through the house, past the bedroom and into the bathroom...he figured if he were quick enough, he could clean up, throw the clothes down the basement steps which acted as their dirty clothing hamper, and climb into bed with Ayesha before she knew of his actions...or lack thereof... approaching the bathroom, he closed the door softly, knowing his minutes were numbered with the door ajar due to the towel racks which restricted it's complete closure...he took off his boxers which were soaked with the fluid fishies he wished he could plant within Ayesha in exchange for a little thun...

...he had the opportunity once and rebuked it...

Now, his moves were gentle and meek, trying silently to smother any damaging evidence, for it would not be believable...and since they couldn't even get through something as simple as what he had originally left for, how would this play itself out...?...he reached in the shower stall for his washcloth, turned on the water in the sink and with the soap began to wet the rag to wipe his genitals, inner thighs and even his knee cap, which had not escaped the sticky solution as his boxers had dropped to

95

the ground...he washed himself thoroughly, and scared to death of the surreal reality of this dream, he would take no chances but instead every precaution with Ayesha's fragile womb, condemned to the likelihood of cervical cancer passed down through every generation of her female family...he slowly opened the medicine cabinet and holding the mirror firmly so as not to have it squeak, he reached for the peroxide...twisting the cap off with three fingers, he held his manhood with his other hand, and over the toilet, poured the cleanser over himself as he held the firing hole closed with two fingers...strategically pouring so as to make it sound like short spurts of urination, he covered every part of himself with the saline...and in an instant, he stopped to debate whether it had been real or not...still undecided, he continued to take no chances, putting down the peroxide and now reaching for the alcohol...he completed the same ritual again...and this time, as he was about to cap and close both bottles and return them to their rightful location, he heard a noise which he thought was probably his cat scratching against the basement door...she always did that...however, it wasn't the she he thought...

As Christian turned his head left, he witnessed his worst nightmare...

The door opened to the sight of Ayesha, who saw him in the midst of ending his actions...

Looking into her face, he saw her eyes slowly peruse him, from eyes to nose, neck to chest...her eyes continued downward...while his eyes were fixed on her's...

She looked at him with disgust and disappointment in one staggering blow that he could not respond to...

…Ayesha turned away from him and walked back into their bedroom…

…Christian stood speechless, unable to move from his footing…

…after all, what could he say…?

…what would he say…

6—Thou shalt not kill.

The Holy Bible, King James Version, Exodus 20:12

6—Equality

Supreme Mathematics

Person 2: ...but you beat him, of course...(?)

Person 1: umm hum...

Person 2: Do you mean, the challenge came just out of the blue?

Person 1: That's right...

Person 2: hehhehhehhahhaha...

Person 1: Last week I received a letter from this...expert, challenging me to a fight. He said people like you and I aren't as good as our reputation. Seems like quite a few people want to see us dead...

Mobb Deep, "I Won't Fall"
Infamy, Loud Records, 2001.

"...Dog I know about death—you ain't sayin' nut'in slick! Empty out on that Fool —clickCLICK...clickCLICK..."

A nd Christian understood that the sixth time God spoke He did, in fact, let him understand...this was the third time He spoke to him...and He let him know that they shalt not kill..."but why...it doesn't have to be like this..." he thought as he pulled on the twisted tobacco ez-wider...a year ago, he had quit smoking cigarettes because Ayesha had asked him to, a resolution they made together... unfortunately, when the time came, she wasn't ready to quit because of the unthinkable instances she'd been through...still he continued on the path, because she asked him to...and yes, he was tired of smoking, but the fact of the matter was he knew she needed it and he didn't...he had already resigned himself to the fact he was going to give that gift to her, because he loved her enough to change inconsequential things in the name of making her happy...because of the love he carried in his heart for her...now he was back at it, reduced to his lowest common denominator through what had become the most unbearable of times...

He sat surrounded by her, in a house that began to speak to him...and he wasn't going crazy, it was that the walls were actually speaking to him...they would call to him and he would call back...and together, this continuum was one he could no longer avoid, no longer sidestep...and in dealing with it head on, he realized he was not ready for what that brought...

"Have you had any thoughts about committing suicide?"

"Yes," he responded.

"Have you actually come up with a plan, have you seen yourself committing the act? How does it play itself out?"

"I don't really imagine it, I just know I got the gun on the nightstand...yeah, there have been times when I thought I could just pick it up and do what I had to do."

These were the questions of the therapist who screened Christian at his evaluation appointment..."I know they need to see how crazy I am," his way of describing it...as well, the intake counselor at the rehab clinic probed with the same line of questioning, after the shrink referred him to rehab because he smoked weed..."I graduated from Dartmouth with straight A's, I wrote a 300-page Masters thesis and gave the Graduation speech...I was valedictorian...and I did all that high...I don't think the weed is affecting me negatively." That was the Christmas talk, as he was frantically yet methodically completing his Ph.D. applications for four more schools...it was now weeks later, though...and because so much had changed, things weren't what they had originally been because of what went down and how it jumped off...

He ran out of the crib yelling at the walls which spoke to him...

"Can I go now...?...you've already left...can I go too please...?...can I have peace of mind too...?!?!...Is that too much to ask for...?"

Chris got in the second car and murked off from communicative corridors quicker than fast...first he drove around the block a few times...after that, he floated to his man's crib—the kat that was supposed to help him find a new apartment...he knew this kat was flaky, but it was a hookup for him...he'd soon realize it wasn't, but only a shortcut he always tried to take under drastic circumstances...and of course, thun was nowhere to be found...so with that, he had to go back to the bane of his existence...the house that knew no remorse...because it screamed to him and at him in unison with his heart, for it did cry out with them...those walls in that house...

He was driving the car, the set of spiral notebooks sitting next to him...they were for her, but she wouldn't read them...as the rain began to pound upon the windshield, his reaction was to slow the wipers down...he didn't really care anymore about how he was gonna make it...he hoped the notebooks would be okay, because they needed to make it...he, on the other hand, didn't...he wanted her to have them in his death because she would not take them from him in life...as he realized he couldn't see anymore, he told his mother he loved her...and he told his whole family to pray for him, but he wasn't scared because he knew that Deem and Nana and many others were waiting on that side for him...and as the showers began to pour, he left the wipers on the slowest interval, leaving him with only brief scenes of clarity through the oceanic onrush...he let the wheel go as it will, and combined with the rain, his car began to spin outta control until it spun through the dividers...swishswish...and

spinning onto the other side of the highway...
swishswish...spun into the oncoming truck which spun
into a jackknife to avoid the inevitable spin of ceased
suscication...swishswish...and upon the crash he jumped
with a body spasm that left him sitting in a running car
that had never gone anywhere...

It had been five weeks to the day that she was gone,
leaving him with no word...not an email or even a
postcard...merely a small note in the envelope with the
keys...the note said nothing though...and an answering
machine message, because at the point it went down, he
assumed she had to do it that way...he had heard nothing
though, only scant responses through his friend who was
now her's...he knew that his only word on her was
through his friend Katrina...but now, as he found out she
was going to Atlanta to stay with her, it all became too
overwhelming...he got word at work when they were on
the phone...

"The reason I kept telling you to call me back in ten
minutes is because I read your email about how you felt
Emory University was calling you...she's coming to
Atlanta, and she's gonna stay here with me..."

All of a sudden, yesterday was now today...sitting in
his chair at his desk, he folded immediately as his chest
cavity deflated instantaneously...his head at his knees,
perforated at a line which had lost two entire beltholes
worth of waist-weight, he held his head on each side with
the long and wiry fingers that were large enough to easily

104

encapsulate his entire cranium, with the hopes that his brain would not expand and explode from within his skull...the words from his friend slayed him...in the same way her departure did...he had received an email with a prayer he had to send to seven people to bring forth a miracle...and when he sent it, he really hoped for his miracle to materialize...he never thought it would be this though...

Christian sat in the house and the walls continued to scream at him...they whispered in his face, they blew in his ear...but the pain came from how they looked at him...and they sent his psyche into a frenzy...for he was a scholar, disciplined in the archery of academia, yet a writer, with a creative energy that emanated from a place he had been destined to rep for a long time...and it was this fatal combination that fueled his mental, his verve so vivid, his brain would move marathons per minute, causing his emotions to overtake him and oppress his efforts at rationality and rebuilding what now had been destroyed...for his one plus two did not make three because when Christian was given Ayesha, they somehow collectively built to destroy their *understanding* on more levels than anyone but Ossie and that percentage could calculate...but there was nothing he could do...and the leafy greenery which once helped to slow his brain down, only escalated the velocity of his thought...and he knew she was not coming back...yet, he didn't and felt that he couldn't do it without...

Christian knew he could give his manuscripts, both written and unwritten, to his man P.eye.P...thun knew his vision, and would make sure it came to fruition...his Uncle Simon down South who had put him onto the science of life with music would get the turntables and the records...he wanted both his nieces and his nephew to have the dough—what little there was of that shit—so that maybe if it amounted to anything by the time they were twenty-one, at least they would catch a little dough from their long lost uncle...he would leave his mom a note with Katrina in Atlanta to make sure she knew he loved her with all his heart and soul...he would apologize to his dad for not going the extra mile he had not been able to go, in knocking out the Ph.D. and being the first doctor in his family...he didn't know how he would explain it to Emil...not after Deem...but he would want eM to know he tried to hold his head, but when it exploded, there was nothing he could do...he had tried, "for real dun, I gave it all I could, but I just couldn't maintain no more..."...the words for Kila and Ossie were still ungraspable, because he knew they would understand, but he would want them to know he loved them...he wanted his friends to know, but he knew some of them would be fucked up, not expecting this, because he was better than that, smarter than that, and really stronger than that...and they couldn't see where he was, as much as they did...and Ayesha, he would ask Katrina to sit down with her and explain that if she couldn't hear him in life, please read him in death, so she could know where he was with her, stuck without any

106

way of communication...he didn't want to hurt her...it was just that he didn't want to hurt anymore...and if she could read the words, they may not be absolutely right, but they would be as much as he could bear in order to get her to understand how he had been broken down to his lowest common denominator, his weakest and most vulnerable form...

Christian guzzled the forty of danney in the whip...the gat sat in the passenger side..."I'm sorry about the mistakes I've made...I am only human, but regardless I should have made better decisions...ultimately, they were mistakes..."...he was drunk in his pain, and as he continued to pummel his person with poison, the gat began to guide him...he cocked the gat back, while frantically writing his last words, his final testament...and after he had finished the forty, he apologized to her...because he didn't want to hurt her...he just didn't want to hurt anymore...sitting behind the driver's seat in the pitch black of night, he picked up the pitch black steel and with one squeeze, opened his mouth and pitched back to the essence of life...and when the gunshots stampeded in the TV shootout, he woke up and realized he had to make some sort of move..."Why the fuck am I buggin' out like this...CAN'T YOU LEAVE ME ALONE NOW...?"

Christian got up off the couch and tried to walk around the crib, maybe some motion would take his mind off where it had gone...he knew he couldn't go to that place, but now he wasn't sad, nor was he depressed...he was tired...Christian had lost his fear of death because he knew

107

when He felt it was time for him to go, He would take him...and Christian would have no choice but to go with Him, if He let him...and anyway, his peoples was on the other side...they had left here and were now there, and if he was to go from here to there, at least he knew he had enough clique to hold Heaven down...the same way his peoples used to rock from Spafford to Rikers, Clinton to Bedford...the more the merrier...that was the greatest factor in jail...but for him, it would be the least to think about in death...he didn't really understand why he was going to this point, because on the real, he was a smart muthafucka...and he wasn't cocky, but he was blatantly honest when he went in the bathroom and looked in the mirror saying "I'm a bright kat...and I gotta do some shit to rep for my dogs in the hood...'til the day they lay me down to rest..."

And he could only make guarantees here, because he had already sold the gat to Ossie...but there'd be no telling if he hadn't...that's how he knew he was smart, because he thought there might come a day when he was here...it was just a contingency plan though...he never thought it would come to life and breathe her sweet breath in his face...it was laced with her like the dust in thun's last weed...it was covered in her like the blood on the Tims of many a Badlands mobster after the usual friendly neighborhood stompout...it was cloaked in her like the deceit, lies and turmoil that surrounded the atmosphere he had created...he turned the faucet on, cupped his hands and began to violently throw water in his face, as if he could wash the thoughts away like grease on his lips from a good fried chicken meal...he washed once...and he thought if he had gotten baptized this past weekend, maybe He might have washed it away for him...he washed twice...but this tap water was far from holy and sacred...and when he looked back in the mirror, he was walking in the forest...the knapsack on his back contained the critical pieces he knew would get to his family once he was found...he left all the important notes...he gave all the necessary reasons to all the important people, and in his writing, they would all begin to realize his walk through the flaming foyers of hell were more than just "...getting over it..."...it wasn't that at all, and she was probably the only one who in her heart knew that...he had finished his chase of Ayesha, yet she would not let him catch up to her...she wouldn't even let him get within a block's radius of her, and so with that, he was chasing an infinite void which would never be captured, slowed or even seen...and now he would throw it to her in death because she would not catch it in life...he stole the heater from his man Ossie who he had originally sold it to...he knew thun would not just give it up to him, so he had to git him for it...after all, it was his though, right...?...and he could no longer bare the swarm of slip-ups he enacted upon her...he could not make peace of mind and ultimate sanity with her, so he would no longer hold it...and while he had taken it to the Highest and Utmost in prayer, at this point, he not only rebuked his plan, but he could not see where He was making it right...he didn't understand that His plan had not been illuminated to him yet, but he didn't have enough patience to sit and wait...he hoped he could be forgiven for that...but he knew He might take some issue with it...another decision he was going to make knowing very well it could be yet another mistake...but humanity would not let this human make it through this time looking humane...because as he lifted the gat to his temple, with eyes outstretched like filaments in light bulbs popping from light to dark, he yelled his life into death beckoning the one in death that held him down in life...

".........DEEEEEEEEEEEEEEEEEEEEMMM........."

...POP...

Christian opened his eyes as his head hit the faucet, water splashing all over him and the sink...he looked at himself in the mirror...but he didn't recognize the person staring back at him...he couldn't even push the tears out right now...he didn't know he would be able to run rivers of tears tomorrow...

Trying to clear the air of his mind, he walked into the kitchen, and in the drawer under the dish drain, pulled out the long knife...this was the sharp knife dresser...he had no gem stars — she had taken her razors with her and the butterknife just wouldn't do...he looked at the blade of the knife...then he ran his thumb across it, to make sure it was sharp enough for it to be quick...he had no can opener to sharpen it up, but it was good enough to do the job he needed to do quickly...and he knew he would be making her mother happy, probably even the rest of her family...but for him, he felt his life was an even exchange

110

for the restoration and repair removal left by him on her...he looked down now at the back of his right hand... he examined the tattoo he had gotten for his younger brother the day after his birthday...this was also the same year his younger brother passed away from this world..."...'til the day they lay me down to rest..."...and he really hoped his clique would understand he felt that way...this time he quickly ran his thumb across the blade as the quick slice of the knife let red run fervent through his skin...he turned his hand over and analyzed the design of his palm...and then quickly perusing the bracelet on his wrist he had taken from his mom, the salty fluid flew quick from his eyes as his quick utter uttered "I love you mommy"...and relinquishing the status quo, he fell through quick sand quick as he sliced his wrist quick so as to not quickly stunt and turn back...and since he couldn't click he quicked and slit the other...he thought about his college dorm Resident Advisor training his last year of undergrad...he was co-president of the R.A. Association, and in one session, he told the resident college shrink not to make light of people wanting to slit their wrists, because it wasn't a light-hearted or funny situation...he didn't know then his brother would be caught quick with a click...nor did he know he would be quick to slit...he walked a few steps and with that dropped to his knees...only to realize he had fallen in the dining room, over a set of empty Xerox boxes he had brought home from work to pack for his move...

He went into the bedroom, and with his spiral, began to incessantly write with the thumbs whose flesh was raw

111

from hangnail-biting writer's block and pen friction from the speed at which the cursive splashed ink within the papers lines...he focused his attentions here for the time being...but when he completed the vent session which would one day turn into his most valued work, he began his Bible reading...exhausted from his brain, its work and its motion, in an instant within reading three verses, temptation punched him in the snotbox, and with that, he passed out, dropping the Bible...

Christian found himself sitting on the ground, looking at the curb on the block...the ambulance was rushing in with police and he could hear his sister Kila screaming her head off...but he couldn't really go to her, because he himself did not know what to do...and he watched as they took him away, and he couldn't bear to see the blood on the wall, brains soaking the paint...he couldn't bear to see the hole in the wall where the slug smashed through reality...

("I've already got two in my living room to deal with," Christian thought.)

He couldn't even bear pissing out the liquor that was plaguing his bladder because he could not bear the site of the bathroom, whether it be the actual room or the act...because he had just lost his younger brother, his heart...why did he have to do it, was all he could think to himself...with all the people and the love around him, why did they take him...why did he have to go by his fuckin' self...?

112

Christian looked up and saw the lights were on and the car commercial that FOX ran on the late night was blaring through the TV...he looked to see what had happened, and when he looked at the clock, he saw it was 2:30am...he got up and turned out the light...grabbing the remote control and turning down the volume, he realized his miracle would be much different...and so much more...almost...he got back into bed...

Unfortunately, now she was going to Atlanta...he couldn't stop thinking about Emory...and he couldn't hold his head anymore...he ran out of his office, and for the first time, he began to cry...kicking the ice that the fluke-fifty degree weather had started to melt, he abused the frozen water and cried while he spoke to her...and he stopped in the middle of the field, took out his rollerball pen, and with the point now unsheathed, he stabbed himself in the left side of the neck, and violently crossed over to his right, blowing his throat wide open for the world to see and hear...and for only the two of them to feel...

He kept walking through the field as his tears clouded his eyes and vision, and while on some level it came and ended quickly, this wasn't one he had to force out...this one came...in the same way it came when he spoke to Katrina and told her he was tired...very very tired...and he didn't want to hear from her about Ayesha...and he didn't want to hear from his mom about her conversation with Ayesha...he didn't want to hear from his family about his mom's conversation with Ayesha's mom...he only wanted to hear from her...all he wanted was her...all he wanted was to reconcile a remedy with her...but he knew he couldn't and with that came the most terrible of pains...because what is one to do when one needs to talk to someone but can't even formulate the words to have that conversation...what good is it to apologize to a person if those words, while wrought with pain and guilt, aren't as heartfelt as one needed them to be...?

Chris loved her and cherished her...yet he knew he couldn't talk to her...she had left him, and until she decided to come back in some way, shape or form, he would not bother her until she hit him...but it was driving him crazy...pushing him off the edge the Furious Five and Rakim spoke of...disorienting his balance on the razor-sharp tightrope he walked everyday in the wrong Tims that were a half-size too small and crushing his toes...it was hard enough as is...and while it was the most unthinkable to take a life, what would be so bad about the fact that he was not affecting anyone...he was only taking his own...?...for even the Bible began telling him that if thee shed man's blood, man would shed him...but it wasn't man whose blood he would shed... "...it is merely thine own..." he thought...and since even later the Good Book would tell him of a time and place for everything, he wondered whether it was his time to heal or kill...clearly he had not stunted or fronted like Hamlet, shook with cowardice of what dreams may come because of taking oneself into the unknown...would he live a thousand nightmares...?...how could he if his peoples was there...?... "...only one way to find out..."...and he knew the consequence would impact those around him negatively ...but only for the fact that it was his own fuckin' life...his and his alone...which he now was without...

He woke up at five a.m., the normal time his biologically conscienced clock had set in his brain since this newfound anniversary—November 30, 2001...the one he had no choice in choosing...he lazily slumbered through the same re-run of M*A*S*H, which was on the morning before...he then got up when the news announced it was six-thirty and he had hit snooze three times 'cause he was already awake...he could no longer justify watching the weather in bed...he got up and did his four sets of fifty morning pushups, a routine he had reacquainted himself with upon her departure...then he took the spiral off the bed and went into the dining room to sit at the table and devote himself to his daily morning ritual of spitting his soul which became encaged by light blue bars and white walls...and when he was finished, he closed the book, capped his pen and went back into his bedroom, laying down to read from the Bible...and when he finished, he came to a critical realization...because this most decapitating form of torture was one he had never known, never seen, and never fathomed imaginable...and while he was not supposed to, he knew he had been to a place where he almost had...and his journey through hell guided by Him and Deem continued...he could do nothing but walk, with the hope that soon would come the glimmer of light at the end of the tunnel...he just hoped it wasn't light from afar and flames up close...he had been there and back...but he knew They were there because They extended him his seventh-fold wish which equated to one miracle...His miracle, was being around to tell this story...

5—Honour thy father and thy mother: that thy days may be long upon the land which the Lord thy God giveth thee.

The Holy Bible, King James Version, Exodus 20:12

5—Power

Supreme Mathematics

The Yearn Burn-ing for the Learn-ing

Yeah, I'm about to sell this car, so I'm lettin' you know now...if you wanna buy it, let me know..." Christian said to his pops...

"Yeah, I definitely want it...let me see what I can do..." was the response he got...

Christian thought it was funny that this wasn't an affirmative action, but instead a potential possibility...it wasn't Christian's pops, but it was the only father-figure he knew...his adopted mother Nadiera never told him anything about the man that donated the sperm creating one-half his lifespan, fifty percent of his existence and person, what made him what he was...part of him didn't even want to know...he figured if that nigguh didn't want to know *him*, then fuck'em...and bloodlines bequeathed this man as his uncle; however *this* was his father...this man was Christian's role model and motivation for continuing through his academic endeavors...and even though he called him by his first name, it was really his father all his life he knew him to be the illest kat...Jerry had shown him the light, the path and the way...he showed him how focusing through school could get him past the projects and break the barriers that were placed before him...but now, it seemed as if the entire equation had gone awry...

"...aight...just let me know, 'cause if you not gonna do it, then I'ma put it in the paper...but I gotta sell it..." the blood-wine-colored hooptie was fully-loaded, a luxury edition in its time ten years ago...and it was a good car even in its present age...Christian had bought it for Ayesha, but now it plagued him like all the other objects that reminded him of her presence, an entity in his life he could no longer work with...and not only did he have to get rid of it for his peace of mind, but he had to sell it in order to get back into his whip...he hid his Infiniti in the garage back at the crib in west illadelph...he had been shifting the flow of funds in so many different directions, that now he had to get back to the essence, the essential bare minimum duties...like making car payments on the Infiniti that was in his mom's name...he had blasted Nadiera's credit with it at this point, and now, he had to do what he could to make it right...he only drove the hooptie because it was economical, and initially, he wanted to have that memory of Ayesha...after all, she might come back...but now, more than six weeks in, he had to make moves...and the money recouped from the car he bought for her would be split so that half would go to the car repairs—fixing the heat, welding the bumper...the other half would go to the loan company to put him up to date and maybe even ahead of the game in his payments as he scurried to pay it off before summertime approached...and now his West-coast Cali uncle wanted it, and David called him at work specifically to pit himself and his drastic situation against those of Christian's surrogate father—this call came from Jerry's older brother, a smooth-talkin' hustla from his earlier crack-days that he reminisced on entirely too frequently in real life for Christian's liking...Chris was hip to thun's

120

game, knowing if he let him, Uncle David would talk his way right back into the theft he committed on Christian for years as a youngster who knew no better...but he was a lotta' bit older...and much more wiser...fifty pounds heavier, and almost a foot higher...and Christian would not be trapped by his uncle's ill-talk game...instead, his concern was Jerry, what was, and was not happening...

The talk of the town amongst Christian's family was Jerry...he had conversations with just about everybody Emil, Akilah, he even tried to talk to his moms, but Nadiera was getting much older, and in her aging process, her ability to handle stress through patience had deteriorated as potently as the refinement of life Jerry had built for himself...no one in the family could touch him back in the day...after Jerry's mom passed away, he moved back to the hood with his oldest sister Nadiera, to help her raise Christian, Emil, Damon and Kila...but there was a method to Jerry's motion absent of madness...for this move was also for him to stash enough money to get his own crib...but when Jerry did it, he went all out...his third car wasn't a car, it was a Beemer that he pushed without selling drugs like the knuckleheads out on the streets...he would float out of the driver's seat and look at them kats with contempt whenever he went somewhere with his innocent-young-juvenile-child Christian...they would cross the street and walk past these kats who frequently sat on the benches right at the entrance of his block...

"What up Chris..." came from the bench on every occasion...

"...yo what up..." Christian would respond, looking at these kats he knew, then sharply turning his eyes down to the ground with each and every step he took with Jerry on the way to the building...he looked down, because he could see them beginning to look off...he didn't have to look into Jerry's eyes, he could feel Jerry's stare scorching the side of his head and burning the ice grills initiated from the bench as if it were another 90 degree summer day with 90 percent humidity...Christian never understood why it was so hot as he could see the frost of his breath bolting downward as he breathed at the ground..."here it comes..." Christian thought...

"...don't be out here messing around with them Christian..." Jerry said in a tone just loud enough not to be heard by the bench-dwellers, but intense enough to ring through Christian's head like a murderous migraine multiplied magnificently as they could not afford Tylenol to treat the pounding...

"...if you ever expect to be something, you'll leave them alone...and I don't want to have to tell you that again..."...but this was not the first time Christian had heard these words...nor would it be the last...

And even though Christian always wanted to challenge this notion for the defense of his friends who were, in fact, up to no good, he knew he couldn't do it with Jerry...because Christian was smarter than the average kid his age...but his strength and security in his supreme mental sharpness was constantly being sewn by the groundskeeper of his budding brain's garden...Jerry was his mentor and his teacher...he was shrewd with an

122

elegance and savior-faire that was untouched by the hood, the middle-class and even the whitest elite...Christian could hold a philosophical debate with anyone any age about any thing, and most times win out with an approach to critical thinking cultivated through actual fact and life experience based in the backdrop of the slums...but the apprentice was no match for the maestro...Jerry not only showed, but proved to Christian with every proper word that spouted from his mouth, with every early morning Christian would awaken to see Jerry hitting the books harder than hard...but that was only the philosophical food for understanding...the materialistic, Jerry had that on smash as well...every weekend would start with the Saturday morning DeeDee-and-Kila trip to the supermarket...before they left, Christian, Emil and Damon were left awake, because Christian's adopted mother— their oldest aunt—felt that sleep was idol action on Saturday...and since Sunday was the Sabbath, all had to be done on Saturday...even if they were only going to sit up and watch cartoons, sleeping all day was not an option in this household during their younger years...and when the women of the house would leave, Damon would go right back to slumber after sleepily saying "eM, make sure you wake me up before DeeDee git back..."

And with those words, he was gone...Chris and eM, they would rush to the living room closet...Jerry was long gone, but his closet was stationary...eM would turn on the lights while Chris would open the door...and the two would stand in awe, as they flipped through every article of clothing as if window-shopping in the smoothest

123

specialty store...Jerry had a collection built for all seasons, Polo for work with the little man on the horse jockeying for position, club poised to clobber the ball...Polo for play, with the signature of this Ralph Lauren character sprawled across everything...he had Guess from his trips to Cali even before the drug dealers in the hood were up on it...there were no sweats, very few jeans, and a couple denim jackets that all carried the four letter P-word...and not nair' stitch of it was fake...on the outside of each closet hung a fur...since Christian was taller, he'd put on the full-length sable...but eM was never mad at rockin' the jet black mink bomber jacket...and they would talk about how one day, they'd be just as ill as Jerry...trying to get to the kitchen, they would trip all over Jerry's shoe collection, which was a blueprint even for Amelda Marcos...Top Siders in colors for every day of the week, Timberland moccasins from the outlets in New England Jerry frequented as a cross-country skier on weekend expeditions with his white-collar white friends from the Philharmonic he played flute in before he got his big break and became conductor...wingtips and dress shoes were the norm though, and not a pair of sneakers were to be found...Jerry was too classy, and if he needed to get real casual, he'd rock sandals in the summer...Christian and Emil looked at one another with determination in their eyes, as they engaged in a healthy competition of pushing one another to the top through their dreams...they would meet there following their own paths, so that while Damon slept, Emil would go in the room and use the double-cassette tape recorder to loop his own beats, and Christian

124

would sit in the living room reading book after book...both of them going hard on the road to the riches paved for them by Jerry...because he was just that ill...

Jerry was the family man everyone waited for on Christmas day, 'cause his pockets, swollen with dead green white men from his occupation at the conservatory for more than ten years, were the ones that allowed him to splurge on his whole family... "...you know Jerry on his way wit' da big guns..." was what the kids always said, knowing everyone stashed the desired goods with him in the family safe-house...he had moved into his two-story two-bedroom townhouse on the white side of town that you could only get to and get let into if you scheduled an appointment with Jerry days in advance...he was the fifth of six children...Nadiera was his oldest sister, followed by David, who now lived in Cali...next came Natalie, then Christian — he was killed in a tragic car accident on his way to Port Authority to catch the bus to Morehouse College...yet another full scholarship lost to death...so Nadiera named her only son after her lost brother...Jerry was next in line, followed only by their youngest sibling Anthony...Uncle Tone moved to London, as he had seen enough of his family's foolishness and the hood...so one day, he said "...fuck it, I'm out..."...and just like that, he was gone...Jerry was the godfather of Damon, the father of Christian, his mother's most prized possession before she passed — the one son who had done it right — two of his siblings were crackheads at this point which was why Christian's cousins by adoption were living with him as the four of them grew up together as brothers and sister...for Jerry's name brought forth an extravagant mode of operation that, as a middle-aged black man, coupled with his comprehension, came a capacity perfected by no one in his family but he...a taste exquisite and refined like fine wine and caviar, ill cars and plush cribs...he was the one, on top of it all...the blimp should have read "...the world...it belongs to Jerry..."

Now with time, age and wisdom, they were all dumbfounded in his decline...and many things changed, like Damon's name...but some things stayed the same, for now Deem continued to sleep...Akilah did her womanly thing, a mother in her own right...Emil had finally blown in the music game, with his dream fulfilled through big houses, closets of clothes so deep they piled up from the floor to the iron hanging rod, and a bank account that matched Jerry's stature ten years before their ages were equal...Christian, he had his masters now like Jerry had his MFA in Music Composition...he worked in a high school like Jerry worked at the conservatory teaching music classes...and Christian, he was about thirty seconds away from taking it to the next level, waiting on the applications to hopefully come back affirmative, confirming his destiny designed through the close study of his teacher...he would make it, forcing the world to call him by the prefix of doctor in a time where this was possible...and he would dedicate it to Jerry, who grew up in a time where this possibility was impossible...but in this present day, even Christian and his siblings resigned themselves to the undeniable fact that even the unthinkable could be thought of and played out... Christian was on the phone, embarking on the usual quest of *knowledge* as he built with his brother-in-law Ossie on the science of life behind the mathematics that Ossie lived and died by, that Christian respected because there was a mystique and a legitimate formula he would express in a different way than all the rappers...

"...I don't understand what is goin' on wit' this nigguh..." Christian said, confounded to conversing in this disrespectful way about the father figure whose fall was continuous, almost reaching below the status he held for his biological father...it broke his heart, but it was what it was...

"...yo sun, I know I didn't really know sun like dat, but Kila tell me all the time how he would never do the things he do right now...back in the day, he wouldn't of even talked to me like he do now..." replied Ossie...

And Christian knew he was right, because before all this, Ossie's persona — to Jerry — was equivalent to them kats on the benches he steered Christian away from...now, Jerry talked to Ossie more gutter than even Chris and eM did...his properly polished pronunciation had plummeted to faulty slang and outdated ebonics that the youth had already invented, ran through and discarded in a hood where the dialect switched up faster than the sun could rise and set...

"You right sun...he woulda shitted on you all day er'day...matter-a-fact, he wouldn't even shit sun, he just wouldn't talk to you...he'd ignore you like a ghost..."

127

Christian replied...and they spoke the truth that hurt and irritated his person more than the needles that embedded the tattoos in his shoulder, hand and forearms for his sleepy brother Damon...these were all done in his loving memory...

"...and I'm sicka hearing that it's fuckin' Deem fault..." Christian said with anger, enraged more than anyone could ever know..."...it's been like five years...we all went through our shit, but now, we all comin' outta that shit...he the only one still doin' it..."

And Christian spoke the truth, for everyone in his family fell in a different way...Christian had grabbed the green Newport box and smoked on the bogies, pulling harder than he did on the blunts, another one of his coping tools he picked up on the path of loss and destruction...Emil killed bottle after bottle of the E-double-brown-brandy, Henney, and any other imbibable intoxicant he could get his hands on...Akilah, she opened up the gates earlier than anticipated and let out a beautiful seed that in birth and early years, was a spitting image of baby pictures of Damon, who was always snapped in shots of sleep...it made some sense later, but didn't five years ago...however, now they were all at different points...Christian had stopped smoking bones and was deading weed through the week, cutting down to only weekends until Lent, when he would cease its calling...eM, he had been clean of alcohol for almost two years, and killed his last album with a sober flow that his family knew he had, but the world hadn't seen or heard until a month ago...Kila, she was working full-time, getting promotion after promotion, moving up the professional ladder at the corporate law firm...they had already paid for her first year of law school classes...Ossie maintained the crib foundation, cashing checks from an ill car accident that spared him, but would allow him to be paid for the rest of his life...and he ain't even really want it...but the monthly checks were crazy, no one would say no to *that* much paper...and they continued to build...

"...yo, you wasn't here, but the last time we was together and shit, Jerry was over eM crib and when eM saw him, he was lookin' real hurt...he pulled Kila to the side and asked her why Jerry had holes in the elbows of his blazer...it looked like thun was really ready to cry...he was like '...yo, Jerry bank account used to be like mine...what the fuck...?'..." Ossie told him...

And it was all truth...Jerry's *power* had persisted, his clarity recoiled into something no one knew...he always kept his life private, which was fine when times were good...but now, times were horrible for him, and his silence stopped anyone from being able to help him through whatever it was that tortured his soul...Jerry had gone from full-length furs and mink bombers to South Pole bubble-goose hand-me-downs...he bragged about his new Jordans, which while new to him had been old to one of eM's partners in rhyme...and Christian didn't think twice about Jerry rockin' his hand-me-downs, 'cause Christian went through wardrobes like switching hood billboards—so quick that sometimes, he never got a chance to wear shit once...Jerry no longer lived in the townhouse on the white side of town, his only explanation to the family was he was suing the house's prior owner and the realtor...and had been for years now, so until the lawsuit was over, he had moved back to the projects with his sister...it was only to be temporary...now it was years...he switched the Beemer up for a fully-loaded luxury Mercury that he no longer possessed...Christian had to drive Jerry in his own luxury whip to the impound who gave Jerry the runaround that Christian clearly understood because he had some trouble with his license...amidst the sheet music and other documents, Christian snatched up the paper with the final words uttered about Damon while he was here, knowing this might be the only opportunity to save that memory...as Jerry cleaned out the car, Christian knew it would not leave the impound with Jerry behind the driver's seat...now living with Nadiera, Jerry had beef with both his brothers and sisters—who were all clean of their vices—and the three young ones now older, because he paid no rent, no phone, no cable and no food...he had converted Christian's room into a junk pile worse than the one left by his off-and-on-again-crack-headed brother David...and while Nadiera struggled to clean the cluttered project apartment, all Jerry did was sleep, similar to the way his older brother did during his white-rock-hey-day

...no one wanted to say anything though...

...but it hurt every one of them in different ways...Akilah wanted to break down and cry when her uncle asked her to borrow ten dollars—"he woulda never did that shit back in the day...that's some shit Uncle David woulda did..."...eM couldn't take Jerry's calls anymore, because all he wanted to do was tell eM how to manage his career which had already escalated beyond the point of belief — and eM had done it not only with Jerry's disapproval, but in the exact opposite way Jerry advised him to...eM could only think of his man who had passed, and the one line he extolled in song about how money and blood don't mix...and Christian, he was trying to figure out how a professor, composer and orchestra conductor who had been tenured at an academic institution for over ten years couldn't come up with $1000 for a car, since he didn't have one now...even Christian forged a way, getting a salary advance from the business office at his job just before the summer, knowing he'd be working a few jobs, and could pay it off before the bills got too hectic...

Every time Christian spoke to his moms, she would cry... "I'm so disgusted with what's going on in here...and I keep praying and it's like God won't even listen to me..."

Holding back his own tears which flowed more from anger towards the agitator of Nadiera's anguish, he told her "...be patient mommy...you too strong for this...the mother I know would never give up like this...you the strongest woman I know mommy...and I love you..."

"I know Christian, but I'm tired...I'm getting older, and I'm getting tired..."

He couldn't bear the sound of his mother's words, knowing that half the battle of age was mental...Nadiera was collapsing in these confines, and with each word, her mental youth began to catch up to her chronological number...Christian could only hope it didn't exceed it before he got his PhD...

And now, as Christian called Jerry from his job, he could take no more...and he didn't know what to say, but he knew the words would come in some way..."...look, I'm about to move, and once I go, I gotta have this car sold, 'cause I can't park them both on the street...I'm not gonna have a garage anymore...so I need to know what you gonna do..."

"You said you movin' by February 1st, right..." Jerry replied...

"...Yeah..." Christian said, confused about the importance of this point...this was Jerry he was talking to...

"...let me sit down wit my checkbook and see what I can do..." Jerry said to him...

"Look, Jerry...I hope you can really listen to me and put the ego aside, because I'm not tryin' to hurt you...but I'm worried about you...you not the kat that raised me and taught me how to live this life...and I don't know what's goin' on wit'chu, 'cause you don't tell none of us nothin'...but I'm ashamed of you...look at how you lettin' your sister live...you not payin' no bills, not cleaning up even a dustball...my mother has to take a bus to Brooklyn to go to the bank because you don't have a car to drive her, and now, when I'm givin' you the best deal I can—'cause I can't afford to give it to you—you have to 'sit down with

132

your checkbook...?'...you have to tell me somethin', for real...because I'm ashamed of you right now...I'm ashamed to call you my father...and I love you with all my heart, but if you don't tell us anything, nobody can help you..."

"...Chris..." Jerry said in a soft voice he always used to cool Christian's emotions when they came to a head, but now, only enraged him more as he knew what was to follow...and as he combated Christian with the memory of his only godson, Jerry sighed and softly spoke..."You know that ever since Dam —"

"FUCK THAT, JERRY!!!" Christian shouted with a rage that led his co-worker to get up from her desk and leave the office they shared...closing the door quite swiftly behind her, she did not want to be privy to what was clearly a domestic dispute between two people who once spoke as father to son, but now, were speaking man to man...

"DON'T DESECRATE MY BROTHER'S NAME... HOW DARE YOU...?...WE ALL WENT THROUGH IT, AND NOW EVERYONE HAS COME OUTTA IT...DON'T BLAME THAT SHIT ON HIM...THIS ISN'T ABOUT HIM, THIS IS ABOUT YOU..."

Christian held his head up with his hand as his elbow rested on his desk...he did not want to do that, but the time had come...and he knew he was not to humiliate but honor his father...for he had been told by Him that the only way his days would turn to nights and days again was to live by this fifth regimen...but as he looked at the big picture, he realized Jerry was disrespecting his sister,

133

their family, but most importantly, Jerry was disrespecting his one and only son...and that broke Christian in a way that only the solitary straw placed atop the camel's burdened back could do...Christian now saw the irony of two number twos catching him when adding one to his *knowledge*...now stuck between a rock and a hard place, how could he confront Jerry...?...and Christian wondered if he had been brought to break with Jerry since Jerry had already broken with his own sibling...Jerry's example was no longer a blueprint of existence...

"Jerry, tell me what it is...because there's nothin' any of us can do unless you talk to us...please, I'm beggin' you..." and this was a clear sign, for Christian was just as headstrong as Jerry, a quality inherited as all he knew in life from birth was instilled in him by Jerry...

"...*please Jerry...*" Christian's voice clearly started to break up as his emotions led him to pull a tissue out the box to soak his tears before they hit his desk and smeared his rollerball ink that smudged when wet...

"...please Jerry...I'm not gonna say nothin' to nobody if you don't want me to...but you gotta tell me...can you hear me...?...listen to whose talkin' to you...you my father, you've been there for me when I could go no further...now I'm here, ready to do the same for you...but I can't unless you tell me something...please..."

Christian waited with the hopes that this would be the point where Jerry would come out of it like they all had...

But silence was the only response to his pleas...
134

4—Remember the sabbath day, to keep it holy. Six days shalt thou labour, and do all thy work: but the seventh day is the sabbath of the Lord thy God: in it, thou shalt not do any work, thou, nor thy son, nor thy daughter, thy manservant, nor thy maidservant, nor thy cattle, nor thy stranger that is within thy gates: for in six days the Lord made heaven and earth, the sea, and all that in them is, and rested the seventh day: wherefore the Lord blessed the sabbath day, and hallowed it.

The Holy Bible, King James Version, Exodus 20:8-12

4—Culture
Supreme Mathematics

**"...what up sunthun, surprise nigguh!/
that's how we pop up on 'em/
you off-point, you die in your sleep/
That's the moral..."**

Prodigy of Mobb Deep, "Hurt Niggas"
Infamy, Loud Records, 2001.

...and name shiftin'..."

Thun came home on al-Jumu'a...and upon arriving back home he walked through the door of his apartment, immediately reminiscing on many a time he had in this house from the cradle up until now...Abdullah Zahir looked around and realized how different things were, but this was not what he wanted to see, for he knew he would have time to analyze his new surroundings...his first stop, the one most necessary, was the bathroom...Ab went into the bathroom and closed the door behind him...he took a deep breath and began to cry, for he realized he was, in fact, home...and with home, came the luxuries he hadn't had in quite awhile...he looked around in awe, and wiping the tears from his eyes, prepared himself for prayer, performing wudu' — water-washing his arms, feet, and face for worship — his next action was to place the prayer rug on the floor and begin to salute The Most High on this day...for while to many in the world this was the beginning of the weekend, the start of the jump-off and yet another end to one hectic work-week, this to Ab was the most Sacred Day...and it was just that for many reasons, the first being Abdullah Zahir was given another day in the world by The Prime Motivator ...and running a close second was he was home to close the door and pray in the bathroom...or go to the mosque, if he chose to do so...after he finished his prayers, he spent an hour on the toilet and almost two in the shower...Ab was ecstatic to be able to shit and wash, bathe and breathe by himself...all alone, nothing surrounding him but

137

solitude...no more eyes to watch and no ears to hear...no more fending off hands trying to touch and no more noses sniffing to catch a whiff to jerk some shit...and no more open mouths obsessing so desperately to taste...while he was in the shower, he began to cry again, for these would be the tears in a series of many that were to come as reality began to set in on him in the most positive of ways...Ab wailed in the shower yet continued giving praises to Him who they were due...and it would be this water that would cleanse and regenerate, purify and rejuvenate his physical form, allowing his mental to return to this most clean and sanctified chamber...but even with a clean external, Ab would learn too late of the most vile of internal locations...for some things did, in fact, change...but some things stayed constant, remaining the same...and Ab would have more than enough time to figure out those details...

...in the meantime, Abdullah tried with all he had to wash away the memories...for these visions plagued him at any given second...and he remembered the night before, how he couldn't sleep, ready to bounce outta his jail cell...ready to rock out in the real world...Ab was a new man now, and the elevated and radiant servant of God was hearing nothing but being most righteous with God...however, even being righteous through Allah, Abdullah found it most difficult to continue to let his spirit transcend the boundaries of the physical...transcend so as to escape incarceration while leaving the body lifeless and limbless to figure out how to put the pieces back together...what they did not realize was Ab had all the

138

pieces together...all his ducks were lined, in one very nice and organized row...for it was here, while thun was locked up, that he began to find his God in the form of Allah in the most peaceful way...and realizing with an informed scope let him escape the way of life that was considered the inescapable...for in the mind and heart, his religion helped him escape mentally through the physical...for the physical was a trap that could not hold his mental...it had once before...but now, since Deem was Abdullah Zahir as Ab, he had a new way of living in this prophetic path to God with newfound life and faith in and through Allah...and he had been released on Friday...his Sabbath day...al-Jumu'a to the Muslim community...just touched down on home ground...that being the hood...and Emil would be the one to help Ab enter reality yet again..."...c'mon thunthun..." were eM's words which brought a beginning to Ab's new reality and an end to his flashback for now...

"...I understand you home...but a nigguh gotta take a shit yo...and we gotta go do somethin' sun..." were eM's words as he stood at the door and counted the five grand he took from the bank earlier that morning, specifically for Ab's welcome home shopping spree...straight up and down, Emil was gonna make sure his brother was right on top and fresh-out-the-box...and since Emil was shinin', every and anything was given to his brother as a welcoming back to the world of the physical his mental had escaped...and on this Friday, Ab let it return to him...and his torture would be that he let his mental return for that instance...

...as Abdullah exited the shower and the bathroom, quick-ass Emil flew in right behind him, slamming the door so as to beat his mother and anyone else in the house to the punch...

...Ab went into the bedroom he and eM once shared, but now Ab knew it was back to the good ole days...for anything that was Emil's was Abdullah's, it had always been like that...this time was no different...Ab dried himself off and praised Allah yet again before he got dressed in eM's apparel, the usual mode of operation before he had gone to jail...back in the day, eM would make a little bit of a grumble, but ultimately didn't care, for he shared with his brother...and exiting the bathroom to enter the bedroom, eM saw his brother getting dressed...

"...just wear anything..." eM said to Ab..."...it ain't gonna matter..."

"...how you figure...?" Ab asked, not knowing where eM's head and pockets were at...

"...thun...you home...we about to go shopping...so you probably gonna change clothes like five or six times...that shit you puttin' on right now sun, we throwin' that out once you git ya' first outfit..."

...Ab saw a look in eM's eyes he had never seen before...

"...welcome home thunnie..." eM said to his brother as he hugged him tighter than ever...

"...we all missed you sun..."

140

...and who would have thought on this most glorious day of al-Jumu'a that Abdullah Zahir would exit the existence that once encaged and encapsulated his essence...here he was to drop to his knees in exaltation as the words rang in the form of three syllables speaking truth in the vein of freedom...with these words, not only had Ab known he was indeed successful, letting his mental escape the physical incarceration set upon him by the enemy...as well, he now realized his most arduous prayers had been answered by Allah...here, his God, The Compeller he Worshipped, had given him his first name, a newfound name, given to him in the clink...here Abdullah Zahir was truly to find a new *culture* bestowed to him from and through Allah in the form of eight letters...Abdullah swiftly dropped to his knees and gave praises to Allah...but who would have ever thought on this most glorious Friday that all this would take place...Abdullah had hoped this day would come...and time had found itself in tandem with his plan, exiting with escape routes via his own mental plan through his God Allah...and like a rag doll blowing in the wind, with the swiftness Ab bowed up and down, giving praises to The Absolute, The One and The Only...The Source of Peace and Perfection...The Irresistible and The Supreme...

...for this was his Sabbath day...in his new spirituality labeled Sunni, here Abdullah Zahir—the elevated and radiant servant of God—was compelled to pray as his entire family began to wild out, knowing it was only a matter of time before they would all be out in the world again...together again...what better way to enjoy the fruits

141

of the six days turned six weeks turned six months three times...the jackpot wasn't the way of the devil, but instead the supreme gift of Allah—Abdullah Zahir's freedom ...this gift brought the family collectively to the end of their long-awaited journey being al-Jumu'a...the Sabbath...even though his mother, sister, and aunt were Christian, his brother was undecided and his other brother was in college, here Ab stood as Sunni...and as a Sunni he diverged from the path his family chose to walk...so while they ceased to desist on Sunday, their day of rest, their day of relaxation, for Ab, this day was Friday...for this was his Sabbath as Sunni...however, he had now reached a point where he no longer had to pray on lock...he really could go to a mosque...any mosque...and not only in the borough, but in the surrounding four or even the greater Tri-State area...for he was out in the real world now...he was now in-tune with his informed sight, and this new technique of breathing day-to-day through Allah led to his freedom...freedom bestowed through the dexterity of Allah, The Almighty and Ever-Present...and Ab realized he had escaped the clutches of the boys-in-blue and the whole penal system...the snakes in the grass that continued to teach falsities and uncivilized ways to his peoples remaining in the hood who were easily persuaded to live the fast life...his peoples that were ignorant to the science of life because, by no fault of their own, they were wrongfully taught and terribly brainwashed...his peoples that straight up and down knew no better...

...here with Allah, Ab stood righteous...a teacher and servant within poverty whose riches were bestowed in the form of freedom...

...Ab would never forget this day, and would honor it in the same way the fourth slated rule on the second tablet would dictate to Christianity...yet and still, even in Islam they found this notion to be a true story, a significant piece of actual fact...and without doubt, just as quickly as Ab acknowledged this freedom, his torture would soon come in how he was to walk with it...

...when Abdullah was finally dressed and ready, it was on like popcorn...for here, Ab was back in the world again...Emil rallied up the troops, and they all went, leaving the apartment and walking through the block to the street where eM's truck was parked...eM threw Ronald the keys so he could open the Jeep for Ab, their moms, and Paul Michael...

"...a-yo La..." eM called out to his man Lymien, who was notorious for being Uncle when it came to dropping wisdom in the form of jewels worth riches through the art of storytelling...however, he was introduced as Cousin after all eM's shows when it was time to talk to the groupies...and before La could even get to eM, Emil had jumped into the middle of the busy four-lane street, flagged down a cab, and was now flagging La over...

"...c'mon sun...I don't got enough room in the Jeep...take this cab and meet us on Steinway right in front of the Wiz near the parking lot..."

La ran over to the cab with both the Twins...and no sooner had they hopped in the plush Lincoln Towncar had eM peeled off a Benjamin Franklin for the driver...the trip was barely worth an Alexander Hamilton...

"...keep the change..." eM said..."...but DON'T lose that Jeep right there in front of you...aight...?"

"...Alright brother," the driver replied, pulling up close, right behind eM's bumper...and as eM's whole clique had perfect timing on this perfect day, eM's partner floated right around the corner and hovered over to the side of Emil's Jeep...Lex, J'on and Eddy screamed out the windows which slowly came down to release a mushroom-cloud of chronic-smoke from the smoke-gray interior of Lex's charcoal-black Lexus...

"...THUUUUUUUUUUUUUUUUUNNNNNNNN..." they all screamed to Ab, who never smiled, but nodded his head, acknowledging his peoples and his joy being back on the planet of The Badlands...

...now that eM had assembled his whole team, he kissed his two fingers and raised them in the air in the peace sign he loved so much, and actually felt in his heart and soul today...and just like a general commanding his first infantry, he let everyone know the orders with only three words...

"...we outta here..."

eM ran to the driver's side of his Jeep and as he hopped in and slammed the door, he looked right at his brother with joy and admiration—emotions they never got a chance to express in the cold-ass world called The Badlands...

144

"…MY MUTHAFUCKIN' NIGGUH IS HOME…THAT'S THAT SHIT…!!!"

"OOOUCH" eM screamed, as Natalie slapped him in the back of the head as all mothers did when the time came to reprimand their child's foul-ass language…

…and for what might be one of the last times, they all laughed together…even Ab…for here he was, back in the world again…

…eM and Lex both parked their cars in the lot a block away from Steinway Street…and just when Lex was going in his pockets, eM shouted at him…

"…uh-uh…don't do that…" and hit the parking attendant off with a green-faced-Ben-Franklin…

"…that's for both of these cars…make sure they not blocked in when we come back…" eM said, as he gave his man Lex a pound, who replied with "…good lookin' thunney…" as they both walked over to their clique which was deeper than deep…eM was glowing…he was the happiest man on the planet that day…after all, who could tell him shit…?

…his brother was home…

…eM walked up to Abdullah, put his arm around his shoulder, and guided him away from all his peoples that surrounded him…

"…this world right here, this shit is your oyster today sun…" eM whispered in his brother's ear…

"...and you know what...I got five g's to prove it..."

eM dug into his pocket and keeping only the necessary five hundred to make it through his daily operations, he gave Abdullah the rest of the wad of green parchment...Ab looked at eM in utter disbelief...and as Ab began to reply with "...look eM, you don't hav—"

"SHUT UP...!...YOU HOME NOW...and I ain't hearing no parts of 'I don't gotta'...take it thun, it's for you...I been stashing dough for the past year waiting for this day...and for real, if you don't take it, I'll give it all to someone right here on this street..." eM replied...

...Abdullah stood silent...all he could do was look at his brother...Ab hadn't seen him in what seemed to be an eternity...and before he could say a word, he closed his crying eyes and outstretched the stack of green in the air and honored The Generous Giver on this day, the Sabbath...and when he was done, he hugged his brother...here they were, together again...and no sooner than they embraced had the God Lex stepped up, palms upright and hands outstretched...

"...Allah U-Akbar...take this offering as a gift from me..." Lex said to Ab...the God Lex had been righteous for years, and was happy to see his clique finally share in the good times, the fruit of their success...

"...Alhumd Allah..." Ab replied, taking the white envelope from Lex...and as he opened it, his five grand from his brother had been multiplied, doubled by the God Lex...

146

...now, Abdullah Zahir stood with ten g's...

"...shit, say no more..." Ab said...

...and with that, they all went on a tear, up and down the shopping district of Steinway Street...for here they were...Emil, Abdullah and their moms Natalie...Lex, J'on and Eddy...Melquan, Melvin and Uncle La...Ron, Paul Michael and even Earl had met up with them, the kat whose skills with the orange sphere were similar to his namesake Earl the Pearl who had rep(resent)ed the Knickerbockers of NYC to the fullest...and like children in the candy store, they just kept spending...Ab bought clothes—three identical shirts at a time, each one a different color, different sneakers for different days of the week...and they all laughed and joked and even bowed their heads to Abdullah, who peeled off green paper for the homeless and even the little kids who were short a few dollars on tax in the store at the register...Ab left cashiers with tips bigger than their weekly paychecks...and anytime Natalie pointed, she got it twice...for Ab could see the blessings...and he would not forget this day was his Sabbath...one he had been blessed on...

...but it was here the blessings stopped...and to this day, no one understood why...

...Lex, J'on, Ron and La were getting hungry, while eM and Ab were still tearing the streets up...everyone had

147

bags they were carrying either for Ab or for themselves since Ab had appropriately spread love to the rest of his team on this day... "yo, we be right back...we gonna git somethin' to eat real fast..." Lex said, as half the clique turned left with him...leaving Emil, Ab, Natalie, Paul Michael and Ron running right into yet another store...and while no one noticed what was going on, somehow, the infantry had been separated into war and peace, with the grimiest of the crew going to eat, leaving the peace-loving kats to their thunthun's continuous shopping spree... Abdullah bought a few more things in this store...he was unconscious to the process now, not even trying clothes on as long as they were XL or better...and as they walked outta the store, they turned and saw a figure who they thought was a ghost...

...funny thing was, the figure knew he was seeing one...

...as they walked towards each other, here was the asscheeks-kat that back in the day thought his gat was so hot, he could spit flames in the form of slugs into Deem's head and leg...and somehow, not only did Deem live to make it through another day, but he also lived to make it through his name shiftin'...for Abdullah Zahir wasn't Deem anymore...

...but this kat, he didn't see it that way...and with this sight, he stepped right to Ab's person... "YEAH NIGGUH...NOW WHAT...?"

148

eM and Paul Michael looked at each other and knew it could not go down like this today...without speaking a word, eM went one way, putting his arm around his mother's shoulder while Paul Michael stepped up right in between this kornball-kat and Abdullah Zahir, the righteous one...

"...c'mon mommy...let's go ge—"
"...who's that...?" Natalie barked, displaying where her sons got their viciousness from...

"...yeah, tell ya fuckin' mommy who I am muthafucka...so now you out in the world and you think shit's sweet now, huh...?...you know you can't stay here for long sun..." was the words outta this kat's mouth...Paul Michael stepped right up in his chest...he grabbed him by the arm, talkin' sideways outta his mouth..."...git the fuck ova' here...what the fuck you think this is, you see thun out in the world wit' his moms...he ain't even thinkin' 'bout you...this is some shit that needs to be settled some other time..." Paul Michael said swiftly...
"...nah, fuck that...y'all call that nigguh Deem, right...?...let him kill somethin' now...now what Damon...?...who the fuck you wit' muthafucka...?"

...and right here, Abdullah stood frozen...

"...c'mon thun...we outta here...we got better shit to do..."...and yes, eM was all too good at talkin' fast to get

149

up out a situation...but he looked in Ab's eyes and knew his words hadn't been swift enough this time...

...Paul Michael kept pulling at this kat's arm, trying to drag him into the McDonald's the rest of the army was in, knowing it would be like a roach motel for this kat...he'd get in...but this bitch-ass nigguh would not get out...but he fought him with everything he had...this nigguh, he felt if he didn't kill Deem right then, then Deem would kill him...only problem was, Deem was nowhere to be found...but the way he was talking to Abdullah and violating his person, no one knew what could or would happen...

...and still, right here, Ab stood frozen...
...but his eyes spoke for him...in the way they had so long ago...

This kat, he didn't even see the changed and newfound actions of Abdullah's changed life which led him to freedom...and with his words, he clearly had reached over the line, disrespecting what in Abdullah's mind was his most Holy Day...his Sabbath Day...the day out the joint ...the first day in the world...his first day out the cage... the day in the light, unshackled, unchained, and able to move about how he wanted...finally, his name was Abdullah Zahir and not Prisoner Number 97D4402...and that was the realness of it all...no more chronic in Bible papers, no more hustling for squares in the yard...no more block-sized-bread and mashed potatoes...and no more showers ice-grilling inmates to let them know it was

150

definitely not bangin'...and what was thun to do now, his moms was there, clear, coherent and happy to see her middle child back in the world again...this was what the Sabbath was supposed to be...celebration and relaxation in the day after all the hard work had paid off, producing the exact extreme of what the family picture in the dictionary for the definition of the American dream should be...and here was this dumb muthafucka tryin' to violate Ab...on some other shit...

...what was thun to do...?

...all his dogs was right there, barking hard on that nigguh...and his clique, the way they got down, was ready to go all out for thun on the day he departed from the dungeon to the Light of the ever-living world...thun was confused now...he had to figure out what to do in this situation...his whole civilization was coming to a close, for as his mental returned to his physical, his physical trapped him momentarily in the same way the jake and the pigs had caught him when he was on the run to imprison him in his physical before he uplifted his mental...now caught up in this real-life-shit, what was it that thun was really supposed to do...how was it all supposed to go down now...?...for his freedom alone let him know that he was indeed, supposed to chill...for that was the exact reason Allah had brought him into and out of where he was...and now look what was goin' down...he couldn't even chill on his own day...and just when he thought he was out, like a fiend from crack, he could feel his mental trapped in his physical,

151

getting pulled right back in, deeper and deeper...and for a split second, when his mother called him, thun was confused and had forgotten just exactly what his name was...because right then, he didn't really know and couldn't decide...for his mother and father gave him a name in the form of the worldly government...the streets gave him a name describing his actions...and then, before the end was at hand, even Allah gave him a name...but now, he didn't know what he was supposed to do...that was the extent to which his mental had been incarcerated yet again in the physical confines of his own life...the one which he willingly walked away from...both in and out...why was it going down like this...?

...and it was here, on this particular Friday...this Most Holy Day...here, when he was out with Emil and they were shopping and wildin' and chillin' again 'cause thun just came home...and with the whole family here, the kat that tried to body Deem, was now coming to step to Ab...

...two entirely different people...

...and this nigguh had gone so far as to step to him while Natalie was there, immediately making a bad situation worse...that was one of the many violations this kat committed in a matter of split seconds...wasn't it bad enough this asscheeks-nigguh's right hand man's testimony couldn't hold thun locked up...?...now, this bitch-ass had to look into the eyes of what was to him a ghost...and this shook-ass nigguh looked only to realize he instead stared at his own reflection...for Ab was righteous and holy...*this* kat was the ghost...and he knew not of Abdullah...but he did know of Damon who Abdullah Zahir had tried with all he had to leave behind...

...everybody around them stopped the situation, but upon just coming out, thun realized it was over...and his torture was he had to flip scripts on what was supposed to be his Most Holy Day...why...?

...why, upon just being released from the cage, was he now forced and destined only to return to it...?...he thought and contemplated as to who he was gonna be right then...and his last words let everyone know how it was going down...for it was over...."...they startin' up again...I can't go through that again..."

...and this would be Abdullah Zahir's torture...for now, he had truly been captured, and incarcerated back into the physical...

...and then time made a chess move...

…and he was responsible for the next…

…he removed his kofi from his head…

.

…and then removed it…

Part I

…and He took me to the mountaintop as He had with others…

…and while alone in His company,
He showed me what this was to be…

…and in His presentation,
He gave to me instructions as to how to convene in
relation to and with Him…

3—Thou shalt not take the name of the Lord thy God in vain; for the Lord will not hold him guiltless that taketh his name in vain.

The Holy Bible, King James Version, Exodus 20:7

3—Understanding

Supreme Mathematics

(ref.) ...see seven deadly sins for solutions...

But for some reason, before he decided to do what he needed to do in his travels through it, he stopped and contemplated what led him to this place in the first...for in this darkness, maybe the Light that he sought could be found...and so, he paused and pondered past passings...

...Christian sat in the apartment with Ayesha and continued with his verbal onslaught, in a constant effort to slay the One he claimed he loved so...and he used Her name with 1/7 of the sins which saluted the concept of solution...and all towards his newfound Savior, because after all, this was who he was serving...sitting in the house with Her, the arguments and verbal abuse was non-stop..."...I hate you...I wish I would've NEVER did this shit with you..."...he blasphemed against Her in arguments, because he would get to a point where he couldn't win, for while worshipping Her, he realized he felt that since he had Her, he could do what he wanted...and so he didn't realize how he had defamed Her, desecrated Her essence in his wicked ways, called to people in spirit who probably took Her because at the time, it was the right thing to do...oh how he changed his wondrous ways he had found in Her...he had Her, and loved Her...but then it went away...because with the breaking of the first, the understanding had to come in the third...so that now, he was lost and alone, because he was wrong, and not held guiltless by Him in his actions towards Her...and the fact of the matter was he made Her a Deitess...yet at the same time, how could one who would act in the ways of worship in one minute, turn into the exact opposite in the form of the extreme antithesis in one fell swoop, in like thirty seconds...?...it really didn't make any sense, but on some level, he understood Her words that didn't come directly from Her mouth, but instead in a message sent via third party...those words were simply..."...let Me be..." and that was the dirt his dirt had brought him...and it felt real weak to be this dirty, believe that...but it was him, and nothing else...and yes, without question this pretentious and preposterous part of him was what inevitably brought him back to Him, so that now, he knew he had to shadow himself within Him, he had to recall his rhetoric in order to wrap it up...the dishonor of devastating spazzout sessions in which the sword he possessed in the form of his words was waged against Her in any and every way, in order to be him...and win...for some reason, that was what he thought the meaning of life was...maybe if he would have tried to walk with Her to the top, instead of slaying and dragging Her consecrated carcass like a caveman, they would have been the They that got there...but it didn't go down like that...from the last time war would take place, to so many before it...it was a wrap he shouldn't have been oblivious to, given the circumstances...

"...look at this shit...all the shit I've done for You, this is the fuckin' thanks I get...fuck outta here...You musta lost your damn mind...who do You think You are, huh...?"

"...first of all, who the fuck you think you talkin' to...?...what do you think this is...?...I don't have to stay here for this shit, this ain't what I signed up for..."

160

...and somewhere along the line, Christian forgot how to love Ayesha, how to live life right by Her...he thought it was doing it for Her the way he wanted it...he should have seen that if he'd have done it through Him in the way She wanted — because he never really listened when She told him how close He and She were — it wouldn't be like this...but instead he did it like he wanted...and now here he was, seeking Him in order to illuminate the science of him being left alone while She was long gone...

"...and you think this is what I signed up for with You...?...look at this...I've done everything for You, I've given it all up...I left my family for You, skated from my home for You...I give You everything, and this is how You repay me...You musta lost Your damn mind like Your moms...guess the fuckin' apple don't fall too far from the tree...just leave me the fuck alone...I gotta think..."

...like full moons cornered in cloud cover, this was the hue he saw and, just as the beast in the man, he howled as he changed...yet Her shades made him see hues in blue, no more pain bequeathed to him in bloody crimson...so blue, even he felt crypt-ed out...his slander stuck him in this murderous mindset...and now, when he saw the moon, he longed for Her Hues, he yearned for his Sun...for She was that for him...but wasn't he supposed to be the sun his Earth revolved around...?...where had he gone wrong...?

"…fuck that, I ain't leaving shit alone…!…you gonna deal with this shit…and right now…"

…he looked at the gat that sat on the table…and he could feel the grasp he had on his mind slipping away…he blamed that slippage on Her though, not realizing it was, in fact, him that was slipping off the edge and into the brink of insanity…he put his elbows on his knees and cupped his head in his hands, trying with all he had not to let it explode…and She stood there, he could feel Her presence…and as his head continued to pound, he spoke to Her again, because She would not listen to what he had said… "…did You not hear me…leave me alone…I need to think…please just leave me alone…" he said to Her softly, knowing with every word to Her, he was losing more and more of his sanity…

"…I ain't leavin' shit…so now what the fuck you gonna do, huh…?"

…He allowed him to see Her…in the flesh…He blessed him with Her face and Her gracious glow, whether in the pale-skinned dead of winter, or the light brownish olive natural toastiness of tans in the summer…the hair that changed life and color through seasons, so rich in a summertime shine of autumn auburn tones…the Face that could not be seen by anyone or thing other than as timeless in a nature that could not be described here in words…but Her Eyes, how he loved to look in Her Eyes, because Her's were the only Ones he thought knew him…Those Eyes were the only Ones he could look into and never be afraid

162

of…and he sank, lost in the tunnel he traveled down at one point together, for the brown, that Brown, was One he would never forget in his entirety…She was perfect, there was nothing else that could describe Her…he was enveloped in Her ethereal epitome…so why had he executed Her edifice…?…Her angelic epiphany blasphemed in effigy…

…he picked his head up and opened his eyes…and as his head continued to pound, his first sight was the coffee table…and the first thing he saw on it was the gat…he had a license to bear arms in his fortress to protect his home…there was no reason not to give him one, he had no felonies, his utmost violations were speeding offenses…but if they knew this was coming, they probably wouldn't have let him walk out the shop with both pistol and box of slugs…and She saw what he saw…

"…what the fuck you gonna do, huh…?…you lookin' at the gat, fuck you gon' do, shoot Me…?…ga'head…you think you gonna gain stripes for that…?…ga'head then nigguh…SHOOT Me…please, I dare you…"

…and She yelled back at him when the heat was on, because being headstrong, She backed down to no one…this was what led him to this tunnel, and what would become his torture…and similar to how He gave Jesus, this was almost His notion to him…this was Him giving him the attainment of Her because He and She were close, and She was to him as what He gave the world in

163

His Only Begotten…and he had sent Her away not knowing in doing that, he sent both Him and Her away, but He returned because He gave a promise that He would to any that asked…but His work in granting Her back to him, might really and truly not be a possibility…

"…now look…this is ALL Your fault…fuckin' bitch…"…he screamed at the top of his lungs at Her as he attempted acts of assassination against Her character…with every word and deed…so in spirit, She separated, taking his with Her because of his word and deed…and in moments of derogatory sobriety, he was calling in favors and then, not only desecrating Her afterwards, but basically desecrating those who he had initially called in the favors to, including Him, because he was really supposed to be calling them in to Him and not anyone else…

…his head wouldn't stop pounding…
…and the gat started to call him…

"…what type of God would put me through this shit…" he whispered to himself…he was losing his mind here…and time was indeed running out…and his head kept pounding…

"…please just leave me alone…" he said to Ayesha softly…
"…no, fuck that…you a grown-ass man, deal with yo' shit…or maybe you just a boy frontin' like a man…maybe I need to go find a real fuckin' man…cuz you ain't that…now what…?"

...those words were the last of the pounding in his brain, the last solitary swing of the sledgehammer upon his cranium...Christian picked the gat up off the table...

...and if he would have let Him shadow him, He would have shadowed Them, so that he and She would have been a They more so than he and She were...not only would there have been Another to lead he and She to They, but there would have been the workings of Him coupled with the acknowledgment of the understanding that would have kept he and She as They and not he and She...he had ruined the She He had given him, and now, he had to figure out how to travel solely through the tunnel he began to move through as he was left to seek Him out...

...for She busted gats for the sake of Her own well-being, in defense of the one thing She owned entitled life... he busted gats at Her for the sake of stupidity, trying as hard as he may to be hard...and not only hard, but harder than She...the words in his mind yelled to and at Her, through degradation and other negative connotations because he was trying to win...for everything was a competition...but in the end, all that was left was the chess game he played with time...and even though She may have retreated, he had to ask himself who really won...?...and it was at this point when he realized this was not how it was supposed to be in life, in love, or in his motions, actions and reactions with Her given by Him for him...

"…oh WORD…that's what it is…?…then ga'head, shoot
Me …I dare you…you ain't gonna do nufin with that shit
…you think that gun makes you hard…well how 'bout this
…fuck you…ya' bitch-ass nigguh…lemme call one of your
peoples, maybe they can show me what a real man is…"

…and as quick as She said that, he lost his mind…
…and as quick as he lost his mind, he instantly
cocked back the hammer…
…and before She could even see, he closed his eyes…

BLONG

…but he was always too little too late…for now, on
some level, he truly blamed himself as he questioned if his
horrible and degrading dirt from his front had rounded
three corners, hurting Her around the fourth in it's chaotic
and kinetic karmic comeback…because it was said to do
that…he held a venomous tongue that struck like an adder
against Her friends and fronted on Her foes…for when
blasphemy comes, it takes on many shapes and sizes
besides just a foul word or two…and even with that, now
he thought of counting just those…He let him see
now…that alone, was entirely too many…much too
much…

…he let a warning shot off into the ceiling, warning
Her he was not playin'…

"…please, leave me alone…" he spoke softly, letting Her
know he had now truly lost his mind…and could no

longer maintain and couldn't even see how his blasphemy here had taken on a new level...here, he had blasphemed against Her most prized possession...Her life...

"...what, I'm supposed to be scared of that...?
...word...fuck a warning...ga'head and shoot me...where's the phone at, lemme ca-"

...and before She could even finish that fatal sentence, he now lowered his arm...and without even looking, he let off twice...

BLONG

...once into the wall right past Her...the slug – entitled false wisdom — clipped Her shirt that blew in the wind as She just barely sidestepped in time so the shot would miss the left side of Her abdomen...

...but he wasn't done...
...for now, his arm continued to move down in a sweeping motion...

BLONG

...now living in this house alone, his ghetto psalms sang different tunes as he was left to wish like R. Kelly...for all he wanted to do was talk to Her, be with Her...somehow...he could not think of a way though...he was even stuck in old school like Keith Sweat knowing that his blaspheming and his foul-talking explained exactly how there was a right way and a wrong way to love someone...Aaliyah told him She was more than a woman...and with the lack of silence, he descended alone, only with his own thoughts...for his premises was no longer his...and here he was...and now in solitude to prophesize his pain, he heard Her voice sing with Brandy...for as he always made things about him for them, She constantly crooned, questioning what about Us for the sake of Them...?...he could not see Her foresight in this matter...and without the steadiness of his Wisdom, how could he move forth with Her in birthing a seed called understanding...?

...for he had rebuked Another when the time was upon him and Her...

...and now, given all that his actions ignorantly asked for with both Her and Him...here he hailed in his hurt-harbored hallucinations, hazy yet hedonistic in his haunted honor...or lack thereof...but in these psalms of the ghetto, even MJ spoke of the butterflies inside of him bestowed by his own Butterfly...and just like his clique, all he wanted to do was touch and kiss...and his wish, which didn't come true on most occasions, was that he could be with Her tonight...for Her name is what She gave him...inside...inside...inside...yet, with all this around Her, She cracked the cocoon, spread Her awakened wings, and left him there...and here he was...

...it was only later he found out She was stuck in old school too, on some Karyn White-while-She-did-love-him-She-could-no-longer-be-his-SuperWoman-type-shit... and He didn't blame Her at all...funny thing was, neither did he...instead, he began to reflect and acknowledge the understanding of the fact that he had no reason to...as hard as he tried, he came to a point where he couldn't be mad at Her...for what...?...and in those twentytwenty ways that always come through like either the old chronic spot or in hindsight, he realized it was not Her at all, merely him...and he was alone now to live with that...so he had to call it a wrap, because that's what it was, and what else was there for him to do...?

...he let off at Her again, and this time, She had to jump back to avoid the slug from sinking into Her foot...the third slug called true understanding...the Perception He gave to Her...to realize it was time to go...this one lodged itself into a stack of books, stopping in an old anime graphic novel about a crooked yet moral cop...

...how ironic...

...what he hadn't realized was He was trying so desperately to hide him in His presence with Her...He had given him, this adam, His Eve...and placed Her with him in order to hide him in His Nature and Spirit...but alas, those who are known to go against the grain, that most devastating notion encapsulated in number three, would be led to understand what he did, and he would not go unpunished for his actions towards Her...for while He tried to hide him, he kept showing up in His place, which negated the plan in motion set by Him for him and Her...and so because his blasphemy through Him equated in his desecration of Her, He gave Her His Word and with that She skated...bounced...like a ghost on the third day of faulty fallacies through the force of his sharpened tongue, She rose right up outta there...for if he would have been aware of his next step with his Wisdom, he would have attained the next step of understanding...understanding that his verbal corruption of Him was slanted to Her and He would have no parts of what he had become, even though He did...and so, in an instant, like the Thief in the Night that He had been known to be, He took Her from him...escorted Her out in the world He made that, even as cold as it was, would be warm for Her because He had seen enough of him being cold...of him freezing Her out...of him verbally molesting Her sanctity...of him outwardly obsessing about the ways of the world that were not for Her...

...She stood there, motionless, mouth wide open, staring at him...

"...please leave me alone..." *Christian* said softly to Her...but this voice She had never heard before...the crazed and deranged sound of soft silence yet sadistic

senility...and when he looked up at Her, he saw the utter
shock in Her face...

...and She saw the disconnect from reality in his...
...it was done now...he had cursed their dwelling,
cursed their foundation...but most importantly, he had
vehemently cursed Her...and this blasphemy of his would
not go unpunished in the slightest...he would indeed pay
dearly for this reaction, regardless of what Her actions
may have been in Her Word...his deed here was
unforgivable...so He packed *Ayesha's* bags and showed
Her the exit...

He had made a place for both him and Her through
Him because He so loved both him and Her...but when
the snakes and the serpents, the devils and the demons,
began to demonstrate their desire to destroy him, he could
not see and let them work through him, thereby thwarting
His placement of the space for both him and Her...so not
only did He banish both him and Her, but in that
dismissal, which he had done to Him on so many
occasions at this point, separated all that had been *built* in
order to *destroy* the demonic destitute inside of him...and
He didn't need Her to be there for that...so he would now
be here by himself...and this would be his torture...
because he decided not to let Him be present so he could
be shadowed...but to be quite honest, he told Him that as
long as he had Her, he didn't need Him to show up...he
just wanted to be the key to the lock and the solution
found in the seven sins, humoring his own self in the fact

that it wasn't He who brought Her, but him…still he heard not what He had to say…his illustrious ego-centrism lead him away from Him…and later Her…how humble he was now, knowing He and She both would have helped him; however, he was not humble enough to hallow himself in Him then…he instead hallowed himself in Her…and he knew that, but what must it have been for Him to tell Her that She had enough…?…it would be his own verbal masturbation that would leave Her draped and drowned in the disgusting discharge that he himself had become in his divine derailment, done in by deceit, defilement and dubious dejection which held him…He would do nothing for him now…clearly, She had to go…and He was okay with that…

…so now, here he was…while He was with Her…his torture was he now knew He was here with him too…still…nonetheless…

…here he was…

…and he asked Him exactly how many more times would he be tortured…then, he stopped and thought, realizing that even His Only Begotten was tempted thrice…for him, this had only been twice…he would now keep his eyes open to Him and those who tried to defy Him through him…for how long would this be his torture…?…He knew this sequel would double up in it's trilogy, different from that of His as well as that of his first…that which he had lit three candles to…

...unfortunately for him, this was not His time to let him remedy this...

...in any way...any shape...or form...

...and he cried what he thought would be his last tears for Her...uncontrollably, he couldn't stop what he had wanted to come out for so long, when it was time for him to move and vacate the apartment premises that once belonged to him and Her, but was now solely his...it only came when his people let him know it was time to move the bed he never wanted, yet paid for...and now, he couldn't bear to part with it...and he couldn't even tell Her his pain, knowing full well it was his now...and his alone...for even surrounded by his friends, all he wanted to do was tell Her how sorry he was...but in his agony he knew his pain was what his blasphemy had put Her through...and his words were still not worthy, worthless in fact...it wasn't emotion, it was indeed pain...his ill words and foul tongue had sent Her away, allowed Her to leave him...and he was ready to check into the insane asylum he told Her that Her moms needed to go to...and he had run the gambit, his emotions had taken him around the world, through hell and back only to leave him in hell to traverse through this alone...nothing mattered anymore for the pain he felt was his to handle...his and his alone...he had already inflicted this indictment on Her...and so, even surrounded by life, alone he remained...there was no solution...only torture... muthafuckin' torture that nigguhs didn't, in fact, know...

and here he was...in an empty kitchen that screamed Her voice at him...in a cluttered house which used to be Their home...he *built* it with Her...and along with the construction of it, he knew he *destroyed* it...along with Her...and all he wanted to do was have his words right to talk to Her, to answer the unsolved mystery in the form of unanswered questions that plagued his brain, tormented his entire existence...but he knew this would come no time soon...for as what goes around comes around, through Her, he felt Him explain the come around from all his go-a-rounds...

"...it may never even happen at all..." he thought...

...but maybe, just maybe, He might grant him that...

...but He had made sure he would not go unpunished...he knew that...and so with this punishment, he stopped... here was his torture...

...he was alone...

...sobbing in a bedroom, echoing empty except for him and this bed, he dissected his remaining physical trinity and sent his only two friends away...he bagged the bed and boxspring by himself...he would not let anyone touch it...for here it was, and so in it's comeback, he'd do what he could...for that was all he could do...what else could he do here...?

...where he was...?

...and if there was one thing he would do, he'd analyze much more thoroughly, and listen for the signs much more carefully...because he now realized the first and the third time he had not listened in the way he was supposed to, as He had told and taught him to...maybe that was why He took Her away from him...then again, maybe he just lost Her on his own, since he wasn't moving with Him towards Her, slighting his *understanding* towards his most Sacred Knowledge...but next time, he would listen...number three through the math would follow him..."...thanks to Him...hopefully..." he thought...or maybe this would just leave him to double it up...

...he made a choice...with that, he began to walk through the tunnel, listening for the signs that might come from Him...and he knew He would let him understand the next time He spoke to him...

2—Thou shalt not make unto thee any graven image, or any likeness of any thing that is in heaven above, or that is in the earth beneath, or that is in the water under the earth: thou shalt not bow down thyself to them, nor serve them: for I the Lord thy God am a jealous God, visiting the iniquity of the fathers upon the children unto the third and fourth generation of them that hate me; and shewing mercy unto thousands of them that love me, and keep my commandments.

The Holy Bible, King James Version, Exodus 20:4-6

2—Wisdom

Supreme Mathematics

"...whether together
or...
we...
part...
ways..."

A nd like the Red Sea which was used to part a way for some and compress the chase carried on by others, these were translated words used to describe how this moral fit a timeless story...

"...damn...I wish thun coulda just held his head...if he coulda just held his head for one night...why...?"

Emil continued to ask this question as he quelled the understanding of unspoken answers with his newfound Friend found in The Bottle...he turned It up as he had time and time again, hoping for answers to come yet knowing his Friend was there with him to blind him to them when they broke into his brain and revealed the missing pieces to the puzzle everyone around him had to put together in their own individual ways...he continued to pound away at the gray keys, and holding his own head in the present like he knew others hadn't in the past, between the swallows of the brown brandy tongue-kissed right off the mouth of The Bottle, he pushed through his work, which allowed him the luxury of being this disconnected from his reality...

179

"...all by myself..." he thought...

There was one exception though..."...at least I got'chu here, you unna'stand a nigguh pain..." he spoke as they caressed again and again...his system was so strong now, he had cleared the phases of balancing the scales...before it used to be coke and just a little bit of e&j...this turned into coke and e&j...which would later turn to e-double and coke...and after skipping through the e-double with a splash a coke, he began to wonder what the splash was for...that was just extra money spent, four or five two-liters of coke was a-whole-nother-bottle...and while his name born understanding, he was subsumed in a downward spiral of spirits in the form of fluid that flew like the whirling water whisking down the drain after a long hot bubble bath...and the understanding of eM's most terrible nightmare still hadn't let him escape the fact that for some people, they got a chance to wake up when the realness seemed to reach a hallucinatory head...Emil could never wake up, nor would the one who left him in the blink of an eye through the righteousness of his own name...and maybe there was a reason...but it wasn't good enough for eM...and so he sought his solutions through other means that would inevitably bring about equal ends if he continued on this road...

And now, surrounding by the sown seeds which bore the fruit of his harvest in labor, he had done it...eM had achieved what he set out to do for years...but now he realized money did not solve a single problem...because now, there was only one he wanted to share it all with...but there was nothing he could do...so instead of enduring it, he spent that extra cut on the act of annihilating any Alcohol left in his path...Emil had made it to a certain plateau in his career...he was well-known worldwide for his dark and dreary music that made all his fans feel some type of way...sometimes, he'd pound the pads and play perfection in sultry soundwaves that would make the murderer use that track as an excuse for committing malicious mischief..."...if thun hadn't made that beat, I woulda never did nufin like that..."...his partner described it best when he explained it as his doped-up drug music that was therapeutic to the user...and sometimes, eM made you wild out and slam-dance to it...sometimes, eM made people wanna go out on their block and air the whole shit out with a fresh-new-tech-nine lined with bullets in the clip right out the box and ready to rock...other times, he would bring you into a small crevice of his mind, and with that pain, capture salt in the form of fluid through eyelids that would and could not stop...that was how he got his tears out...because he wouldn't let them out...not since that one day...

Emil had lost his heart and his soul, no matter how wild he thought his heart and soul was...and eM thought about the times when they argued only to come back together the way siblings did...but now, with his newfound pain in the form of loss, eM began to consume Liquor to the point where nothing else could go down without it...and because in his determination he had caught up to his dream and rode the never-ending wave, his lavish lifestyle allowed him this...all he could see was the Liquor...all he respected was the Liquor...and regardless of the circumstances, whether a good day or bad, happy or sad, if there was one thing he knew, it was that he had to get drunk...he had to be drunk...because his whole world had gone insane...and with the e and j right there, he drank away the pain...he thought he couldn't get shit right unless he had a drink...and not just any drink, but a drink to get him drowned in drunkenness...

...and now years deep in it, his *understanding* fell one short of his *wisdom*, kneeling not to Allah but to the *knowledge* that he needed It, he had to have It...and every action called for a reaction...however, his actions became reactions because every one had to be initiated by the poisonous Potion...

...he had to drink to get drunk before bed......and how could he start the day without getting up drunk...?...his desires drove him to drink drunk when waking up......only to drink more...to stay more drunk than the night before...
...he drank drunk through his work, drowned drunk through his play... ...he even stunk getting drunk to pound his stunts, as he slipped off panties and swam through sex...

And while the world around him succumbed to the second philosophical soliloquy scripted in that Stone, he had abandoned all and worked with his new-likk'le Frien'...It called to him...and just when he thought, at times, that he might just be out, It screamed to him, pulling him right back in...the realness of it all was eM could see no further than to the end of the empty Bottle he didn't even leave sips or pour out for any reason other than to top off his own cup...

Mad people in his family were telling him to put It down so he could begin to see the life he was living, the torture he was trapped in...but he wanted no parts of it...for he kept convincing himself that no One who wanted him to be well would place him here with this lifetime sentence to a situation that, at some point, he would have to face...but now was not that time, he had not evolved in his understanding of the science of life...and since he had not yet evolved, he was much happier sitting stagnant in a puddle of his sorrow and his stomach full of his false image of God in the form of his Only Begotten Son—the e-Jesus...this was where he found his Godly image...and banished from the Garden of Eden he had built for himself and those around him, there were snakes that surrounded him, choking the cataclysmic climb of his success like boas constricting his check-out from the cocoon...Emil thought he couldn't excel without It...but what he did not see was his actions while stuck, drunk in deep depression and depraved inebriation...eM even lost sight of the Muslim ways his lost one tried to put him onto...but since he was gone, eM cursed Allah for the theft of his sleepy younger brother...and in thinking it had something to do with him, he tried to make up for the mistake by drowning himself in any and every type of Elixir that crossed his clutches...and even though the brandy was the Bottle of choice, eM could find happiness in the Hen-Rock Cognac, the Lime Bacardi which aided him and his crew in getting bent to crash the party...and don't think that when times was rough he wouldn't take it way back, with either forty fluid ounces of Old tarnished Gold or the Danney, whose alias was a false prophet called St. Ide's...as long as It was there he had to have

It...because he could not have back his brother...but This was as good a kin as any, he thought, turning up empty Bottle after empty Bottle, and then refilling until the next Bottle turned topsy-turvy as serum scurried away from the glass and into his quick swiggin' ass...

And there were some who really knew what time it was, those people around him that tried to look out for him...however, in his dizziness and surreal stupor, he couldn't differentiate between those and the others...fake-ass fuckers they were, using him and his kindness, extorting and exploiting it for weakness...only problem was, he didn't feel right if he didn't have his Dark-Brown-Best-Friend and new younger brother with him...Emil didn't realize this wouldn't bring Damon back, but instead, would only bring him down or bring him back to his brother Deem who was somewhere in death where eM could not be...regardless of his irrational thoughts of objectives otherwise...for eM knew he must live his life and go even harder for his brother...but his Loving Lackey and Leach labeled Liquor had clouded his vision and would not let it go...the Serum he shouted as sacred and praised as perfect would not let his *knowledge* build to his name which born *understanding* so he could comprehend how far he had spiraled down this dark and dreary chasm...for it opened through his heart beating on the gray pads in exchange for musical melodies...he was supposed to bring people there and let them go in four minutes or less...but he never left with them, incarcerating himself fluidly through music that captured the whole world's heart...and even with his washed up wishes of his thun holdin' his head just one more day, it would not change the reality...for his thun hadn't...so since eM could not change the reality, he would use the graven grasp of his inescapable Idol to isolate his eyesight on other things, all things, so long as It took him and trapped him far, far away from that realness he always spoke about in songs...the Liquor would help eM deny his other half hadn't held his head, so now each family member had to hold one-sixth of his casket...and regardless of Emil's singular seconds of sanity which gave clarity, he could hear his family's cries...

...but the Liquor kept callin' him, making sure he wouldn't listen to any utterance other than It's own...and if there was one thing that was true, one person could not tell another man what he was not ready to hear...and since Emil was the type of kat that was gonna do it his way regardless, he continued with this conduct...

And his hot heat in the form of beats bore stars beating down his door just to get a piece of what his thugged-out-hood-anthems had to offer...but for completion and addition to an album, these stars had to persevere...first eM had to be caught, which in and of itself was an unsolved mystery because he went where the Henney took him...he answered his phone when the E Double said it was okay...and if neither One were there, he'd better like his melodic contractor as a musician...otherwise, that artist would either get shitted on because he hadn't had his morning drink, or become frozen from the cold shoulder he was trained from his early days to deliver swifter, disposing of those not necessary to his plan...and most people weren't...eM's brother was, but with him gone, all else was pretty much dead as he was...but success through this first obstacle led to the next...for now, the contractor had to be patient in waiting hours upon end for the hit...for Emil, like every producer and deejay in the industry, always ran late...but since he ran with the E Double, he merely walked as slow as he wanted...and eM was a man of his word, so he'd get there..."...I just hope I got that disc I need..." usually left in the house, now an hour away...the patient payee had better hope he'd turn around...otherwise, it'd be another one of *those* sessions...and even though he could make heat in a hot beat quicker than starting fires with gas and matches, there was always that chance he'd get midway, take a swig and start scratching his chin, rubbing his head and peeling off his shirt...once this happened, go home, 'cause it was a wrap...

Emil was known for his realness which was even wilder with the Solution he kept in his stomach like the full clip in his nine...eM was a star, but humble in his actions and still gutter in his mannerisms...he represented his projects to the fullest, knowing his birthplace was just as wild, if not wilder, than he...the amount of Liquor in his system would let him and the world know who would win the battle of the bloodiest, dirtiest and grimiest...he was a celebrity, who wasn't above pissing in the next star's studio session right in the middle of the floor like he traveled with a portable urinal...and as quick as he completed the raw production of his first platinum single, he would just as quick fall asleep in the booth whispering

186

his rhymes...even the record label couldn't calculate the timing of this genius' gem which would lend to them more money than was cut to him so he could cut it to the Poison...eM would be a rich man if he would have invested in Liquid Stock...at least then, maybe he'd get the Product for free...but until then, it was worth it to pay the price, whether wholesale, retail, or street value on the weekends through the fenced junkyard of the bootlegger, who doubled the price of the E-Double..."...triple that shit for all I care..." Emil thought to himself, for in the same way nothing came between him and the pursuit of his dream, nothing could come between him and the fulfilled temptation and consumption of his Sweetly-Browned-Sour-Nectar...and in the schizophrenic pursuit of symmetry marked by his sign, it was astrology that anchored him as two-face-ed yet balanced...for he would punch his own dog in the face one minute, and cry with that same kat in the next...he'd verbally slay his shorties who he kept on smash...then submerge their heads in spins as if he could not remember the riveting revolt of his prior words...in his cusp of Libra, the Liquor showed the world he had four faces...however, as his two reflected the new two the Brew bestowed, eM knew he only had one...but as long as the Potion pronounced Its passion to him, he continued to make love to Her, hold Her and keep Her inside...in his heart, his mind and his soul...and with every Bottle after every Bottle, he began to do everything in the Name of being bent...his beats had to be bent and backed with lyrics that bounced in the same way...his words had to slur in the Syrup, as he stood slanted behind the mic...he had to be bent to drive, bent to bag shorties...bent to pick up money and bent for brokered meetings at his label so the execs knew if this wild-ass-kat didn't get what he wanted, they would have no choice but to converse with his Liquor and yet another month of delay on the street product that they, the hood, and the globe were waiting on...but for all Emil cared, they could wait as long as it took...when he got it done, they would all get it...in the meantime, though, "...thun...where the Liquor at...oh, y'all drank all that shit...go get me some more sun..." was the command of choice, and eM did nothing but succumb to It time in and time out...and in his torture, there was no known cure for his sickness with the inhalation of Intoxicants...and when he felt like getting bent, he could hear the voices whispering in his ear—"...yo, don't fuck wit' it thun..."—but his nature made him drink away the pain until his brain was numb...and even as the words through his man's beats sang sweet melodies of nothing but the purest emotions of affection... (loveyouloveyouloveyou)...he knew while he was where he was, there had to come a point when he could make a getaway...unfortunately, right now was not his brother's favorite saying that was recorded and played back even to this day...it was nowhere near his "...earliest convenience..."

While in life, his brother gave many signs his end was near, it was only that Deem's words which weren't heard were not meant to be understood...he told his brother's man to make sure that "...you go out there and hold eM down...hold my brother down before these vultures eat him away from his life into death...do it before I do, because if I do, there will not be a happy ending..."...for his name let all know just as life was a given, Deem would take it in an instant with his steel...he would even go so far as to take the carcass from the vultures for them to starve, if that needed to go down...but knowing Deem could not wake himself up from that dream, maybe he began to think he could take something that would shock the world they lived in...

And Emil's swigs swirled his memories into visions he saw, watching his brother as he sat in the apartment staring out the gated window as he once stared out of his cell of four-by-four that he would later conquer in the same way Noah escaped, traveling in two-by-twos...just as this wise world traveler had heard the Word of the rains and the floods, he took a multitude of pairs with him...eM's brother also contained a multitude of verbal markers that would illuminate the science of life he now left as a legacy for all those to see and feel, just in case they were to ever feel the urge to follow in his footsteps...for his nine-and-one-half-sized-Timberland boots were not to be stepped in by anyone around him...that's why he was who he was...for his birth name when added up conceived his being and gave rise to the power he possessed...and no one would ever know how Omniscient Allah would work through him...but for every incident in life there is a purpose to be later understood...his next name came and gave rise to a new phase, for only He knew the reasons that let him live through life not for a lifetime, but instead maybe a reason...or merely a long season...and once he chose his own path like his brothers and sister, his new name gave birth to an elevated and radiant freedom that ironically halted once he chose to build or destroy, to cock and squeeze that first and last time...and his new name slurred in slang would emit the knowledge of his birth, which was bound to death, as the circular cycle would start and subsist with one shot...and before he was to go, his new name combined with the former gave birth to the wisdom of the words used to describe him, bringing him right back to the beginning of the cycle...for now, only He knew why he had to go...only He knew the voices that called out to him, letting him know it was his time...and maybe later, Damon's generational harem, his incited and jaded kin, would understand as all the pieces to the puzzle were put together to be seen clear...in the meantime, though, Emil felt he still was not understood by any, so he chased down Liquor with more Liquor, running to and from answers he prayed his Glass-Bottled God would one day answer...eM still had not received word...he had, though, with every waking day, received the beckoning call to get bent...

...still in all, Allah's elevated exit from Emil's life did not make this math any easier for him to comprehend...

...this burden, was entirely too much for Emil to bear...

...if only Emil could bare the math of his name, *understanding* the new way of life for his family that had been decreased by one...this *understanding* would lead him to see that the *wisdom* of his remaining kin, Christian and

Akilah, understood and operated with the pain and persisted through their own which was almost identical to his...but now, Emil was left without the *knowledge* of *Allah*...so he *destroyed* himself while his remaining kin would cry tears of blood for him with every one of his swigs...

And every time his sister Kila would come to the crib to see him, eM would lock himself in the attic, ashamed to show her what he had become...she was one of two people who would cry while trying to tell him to stop that stupid shit...he was drinking his life away like flushing feces down a toilet drain...only difference was, Emil was worth much more...he was much better than shit, and needed to realize the need to flush that Shit—The Liquor—for with It, all the feces that surrounded his circumference would too dive down the watery drain ...and now, it was only Emil, Akilah and Christian...they had all grown up together with Damon...but now that he was gone, they were all they had left...and because of that, they cried for him...prayed for him...and wished every wish upon a star that he would begin to see the light of day in the form of clarity, and not the light of day in the form of disarray...Kila couldn't take another one of her brothers' funerals, for she was present when Deem was shot and left...this was the path Emil seemed to be walking down...and so she cried with him, at him and for him...she was one of the two...

Christian was the second, for the rest of the family would chit-chat and gossip about it, talking to him in a way that made him feel like they didn't understand his pain...but Kila was there for the tragedy that befell them...and Christian, he was with thun like every day of his college vacations, trying to make sure the unthinkable didn't transpire...and when it did, he cried...and then he got strong...at the funeral, Akilah sat on one side of eM and when Christian saw his brother, who was one of two brothers he never had, his tears traversed elsewhere so he could be strong for Emil...Christian sat on the other side of him...it was just terrible that while Emil had two arms around him in the form of love, he only wanted to embrace his Newfound Friend...he didn't know what else to do, because his wisdom was clogged through suspect cyphers and devilish demons who took advantage of him every chance they got...why should they care, they knew he had it...and they knew since Deem was gone, eM didn't really care...these were the same nigguhs that, if Deem were still here, would've steered clear of eM like the plague...for they called Damon Deem because best believe he would bust his gat over the slightest bit of nonsense...any man who took it to the level of fuckin' with his kin would be laid down by the four-pound instantaneously, unable to rise from beneath the slugs, concrete and dirt Deem would bury them under...the same dirt he now dwelled beneath...but since sun was gone, there was nobody around with that much gangster to scare these snakes and their wicked ways off...

And now, later in time, Christian came to Emil and tried to talk to him about how he needed to stop drinking...too emotional for words, Christian began to cry even before the words could leave his mouth...Chris was

192

stuck, unable to get the words out as eM looked at him half-crazy, half-knowing the pain he felt because the *wisdom* of his addiction was apparent to him...and while the part of Poison pushed him to dismiss Christian's tears, the part of his heart knew he couldn't...because Christian was mad smart, and if he was coming at eM like this, he knew something was up...but just when Christian's words began to sink in, eM could hear the hollering of the Bottle...eM's brother was not afraid to drop his manhood in tears that flowed like a fountain...this pulled eM's heartstrings like his hands pulled his own harmonious samples...but he heard the calling of his name from his Friend that helped him to rebuke his family, rebuke his God, and rebuke everything he had worked for, lived and stood by...eM told Christian he would be alright, but he appreciated the fact he cared about him that much...Christian, too emotional to be seen in this state by anyone other than his brother, left the room to go downstairs and into the bathroom to wash his face and every trace of evidence that he had gone this far into sadness...but before exiting eM's existence, he left him with the only words he could speak without being choked up by his own tears...

"...you don't have to live like this eM...but you have to decide *that's* what you want..."

eM stood in his room, the door open in a way it had never been before...his fork in the road was clear, for one path was to follow Christian down the stairs...and walking hand in hand with both him and Kila, they would take him out of this sick ass life he lived...he saw this exit to his left...to his right, he saw the Bottle beckoning his person...It had just been cracked, almost full, yet only absent of the swig he had taken before Christian came in...

...and at this junction which joined the fork forging two paths, eM realized the time had come...

...and here lied his torture...

...he looked left...

...and then looked right...

...left...

...and right again...
...then right...

...and left...

…and Emil's next look was up to the sky…
…and eM asked Ab what he was to do…

1 — I am the Lord thy God, which have brought thee out of the land of Egypt, out of the house of bondage. Thou shalt have no other gods before me.

The Holy Bible, King James Version, Exodus 20:2-3

1 — KNOWLEDGE

Supreme Mathematics

...exemption from exile in the form of exits...

December 26, 2001
from uncle eM crib @ the glass table...18:26

Dearest Violetta,

It's me...I know I haven't really spoken to you, but I know you're out in the world somewhere...probably with Mommy...and for right now, that's probably best, she really needs you now more than ever...I come to the table and write to you because of what went down today...and I know you don't understand everything, but let me try to explain it to you as best I know how...

I went to the shrink, trying to get my head right...and it's ironic how things come full circle...we were talking about my birth mommy, your biological grandmother. See, when she gave me up, I always thought she didn't love me...but I realized today, her love was even stronger than I thought, because at least she made a plan for me...I didn't have a plan for you though...that's mostly the reason why you're not here, because in my infinite wisdom, even daddy didn't have the right plan for you... and don't get me wrong my dear child, I know that droppin' a seed doesn't make me a daddy...but the love and pain, the anticipation and regret I feel lets me know you're here...and so I must reconcile with you, like I must do with a lot of others...but I'm sure you already know that...

199

Mommy is gone now, at least gone away from me...maybe I should've listened when my mommy told me "...don't buy shoes for a woman, 'cause she'll turn around and walk outta of your life..."...if you only knew how many pairs of shoes I bought her...but that's not the reason...I did a lot of bad things that I really couldn't understand until she left...on some level though, it was best for both of us that she did...still, the hurt and pain is unbearable...but now, I realize I abandoned you even worse than how I thought my mother abandoned me...and that's not even half as bad as how I abandoned mommy — emotionally, mentally and physically...now I can see some of the pain I put mommy through...see, what daddy didn't understand was that mommy was everything...but daddy was silly, thinking the grass was greener on the other side...and in my fear of understanding and dealing with you, I ran away from the situation, because daddy did drop a seed...but the daddy that writes to you now is different from the boy who stood with your mommy as she was doing something I will never be able to speak on, understand or comprehend ...see, daddy wanted his cake but he wanted to eat it too...daddy's brain was trapped in thinking that sex was love and since there was a woman who gave daddy sex at the drop of a dime, he thought it was love...I didn't know then, baby...but I was selfish, I was stubborn, and I was stupid...nymph-manically driven by a thirty second rush...similar to crackheads sucking smoke off glass-stemmed-pipes...I wish I would have known then what I know now...because if daddy was able to understand

200

right then and there, daddy and mommy would be married...and you would be here with us, calling me daddy and calling her mama...and really, daddy should have known from the first time in me and mommy's first house together, when on both knees I cried and begged mommy — the first and only woman daddy ever begged — not to leave because he had done the unthinkable with this blonde-haired blue-eyed woman... and she almost left then...what made me think this wasn't worse...?...and there is really no excuse for the nonsense that daddy did...this is part of the reason why mommy left...because how would she have been able to tell anyone else to stay in her situation...?...clearly, she couldn't...and as I look on it now, daddy would have done the same...still, it makes it no easier...and know that daddy comes from a long line of addicts...you have nanas and grandpas, aunts and uncles, even cousins, who are in some way addicted to a drug, a drink or a smoke...but daddy wasn't stuck on any of these parts of the fast life called the streets...daddy, he was stuck on the notion of having sex...sex with the enemy's daughter...daddy wanted to repay the world that hurt him as he tried with all his heart and soul and brain to just be smart...but in this sick world we live in, my love, part of being smart is being "white"...and daddy was so afraid sometimes to be black...and so he thought if he could crawl up inside of some white walls, he could escape the world and also escape his blackness...and so yes, daddy tried to crawl back and hide in the womb...similar to the one you were forcefully taken from...and daddy thought if he hid far enough away in this white womb, it would take away his blackness...but the last and most vile of times that daddy tried to do this, he knew it was not gonna happen...he knew he couldn't run or hide anymore...but now, daddy realizes how wonderful his blackness is and how absent and void that hiding place was...after all, white is the absence of all color...and black is the combination of all colors shining so bright, they all turn into what daddy's skin looks like...and that's when daddy realized he had to become a man, and stop being a little boy...like how you would be a little girl if you were here...and my dearest child, daddy will never have an excuse that is good enough for what he did, because there isn't one...the only thing daddy can do is live with this pain and stupidity everyday...because know that just because you go to school and do good, that doesn't mean you are smart in life...you can have straight a's in all your classes, but still flunk a class called life 101...and this is what daddy did when your time came...all I can say is daddy truly failed...so not only did I rebuke you, but I somehow convinced mommy to do the same...and I know you have had many more conversations with mommy...but please do not blame mommy...this was my fault...and in the same way daddy wanted to escape his blackness, know that daddy will never be able to escape the shame he feels from this action...

I apologize to you sweet one...I didn't understand until now...and as I begin to make amends, you are one of the first I need to apologize to...I don't know how it would be if you were here with me now...it might be an even worse pain than what I feel now...I'm sorry...I almost wish you were here, but then mommy might have taken you as well, and that I know I couldn't bear...for I know how crazy I was when mommy left me, when we split...but if it were three as opposed to two, I don't know if I would even be here breathing right now...I might actually be talking instead of writing to you...and at the same time I'm trying to subdue the anger and animosity in my heart, I feel as if I'm drawn closer and closer to the brink of insanity...because I am beginning to realize the extent of how bad I was to your mom...and I don't know if I can ever make it right...I'm trying to have faith though that things will work out as they are supposed to...I'm sorry you never got a chance to meet uncle emil, auntie kila and the rest of our family, both sides of it...now, it's so unlikely it rips my heart like gem-star slices over and over again...and I know that you're with uncle ab right now...I hope you can see what daddy's trying to do...I'm trying to get right, and I'm sure you can see if you look into my heart and soul...but know that daddy has come a very long way...and is breaching manhood in a positive way, if he does say so hisself ...that's a joke for you to understand when you are older and can understand all these words...but with every day daddy begins to see things so much clearer...and that clarity hurts like the fiery burn scorching my essence that we down here call the truth...but it does hurt, the truth, if you don't live by it...and I'm trying to do that now...only problem is, it just might be too late...but I'm gonna have a newfound faith in this process and let God and uncle abdullah lead me in the right direction …hopefully this journey will lead me back to mommy and ultimately back to you…for by the grace of God, if mommy can forgive me, I will not make the same mistakes…I will not choose the same choices, nor make the same decisions…by the grace of God my dearest child, daddy promises you that…and I know you know what those words mean to daddy now…maybe mommy will, too…I just hope I am not trapped in this state forever…let us hope together that the levantor will blow the kite back to mommy so she can act accordingly…I know it's hard dearest child of mine…but I will tell you like I told my little niece, akilah's daughter and your cousin—if you pray everyday, and ask for mommy to let it happen, she will hear you…I hope you can do something about it, but you can't even really talk like that yet…I'm so very sorry for forsaking you in this way…I hope you can forgive daddy one day…and I hope mommy can too…in the meantime, I'll do what I have to do to get right so when the time comes, hopefully both me and mommy will be okay…

And believe me, daddy hopes we will have a chance to bring you into the world again, the right way…for the only thing I can say about you not being here, if I even have the right to say anything in my defense, is daddy couldn't bear the pain of you seeing him in the state he was in…there is no way you would have been able to forgive daddy if you would have seen and heard the way he treated mommy…that is something daddy has to reconcile in his heart, with mommy, and with God…for those are the consequences of my actions in rebuking you, torturing mommy and not putting God first and foremost to guide our lives...and everyday, daddy tries to figure out how he's gonna do it...because he doesn't know how he even got this far...but daddy still works for you everyday in that regard...he tries to be that much better, to be that much stronger, to be a man of his word, to be a man period...for know now that daddy has left the realm of boyhood, and awakened in a world where the big boys play called manhood...I love you Violetta...and if you didn't know, now you do...I'm sorry for trying to block you out of my mind...you mean more to me than you know, and I will spend the rest of my days trying to do right by you, for you...and for me...and of course, for mommy...

I love you my dearest baby girl...take care, always look into my heart, tell me what is right from wrong...and if you can, tell mommy I came to talk to you, to visit and say hi...and darling daughter, if you have anything to do with it, please bring mommy back so that together, mommy and daddy can bring you back...never forget I love you...I'll be back to talk to you soon, when I get a little better, and then again, when its time to fly the kite...

I've gotta go now love...I gotta go chasing mommy...

I love you daughter,
Your father Christian

And amazement seized them all, and they glorified God and were filled with awe, saying "We have seen strange things today."

The Holy Bible, King James Version Luke 5:26

thanks...

And for real, please bear with me, 'cause I never saw this one coming...

First and foremost to God, cuz without Him, I couldn't have written a paragraph. To Allah, all of Islam, and every Muslim-especially to the Sunni. The Nation of Islam and The Nation of Gods and Earths—I have the utmost reverence and respect for the ways of actual fact and Supreme Mathematics.

To my whole family, who I can't spell out completely, but thanks—especially to my moms, Ruth Muchita, Betty Jean Mattson, Tameka and Lehman Daste III, Jeremy and Amy Portje, George, Todd S. the first, and Jay Muchita. My nephew Kejuan Jr., and my nieces Anissia, Cee'Asia, Aliyah, Atiya and Miah. Aunt Mercedes and the whole Craig, Muchita, Ellis and Daste family. My sister Nicky, Deanna Cameron and Bill Tinyes-I ain't forget y'all. To "capital H...A.V.O.C."-thanks for reminding me what it means to go hard, and good lookin' out for steppin' up the beat and rhyme game from Juvenile Hell to Kush beyond, for real thun. And really, how could I edit this book without your beats...matter-a-fact, they bangin' right now!!! To the whole I.M.D. clique-Pee (hold ya head thun—we miss you), Noyd, Gotti, Chinky, G.O.3., Gambino, Nitty, Fly, Uncle Lamiek, ALC, and Poppa Mobb—how you do dat there. To the whole Ravenswood and Queensbridge Houses, and every hood worldwide...

To my peoples in Philly—be clear, this is an exclusive list...

208

Steve Sterling a.k.a. StammaRamma, Dr. Al Starr, M.D., Furqan and Joneigh Khaldun- Furqan, good lookin' thun, for real. Zuhirah Khaldun, Mr. George Khaldun (for the wisdom in the intro) and the Khaldun family—especially Elijah, who didn't flip 'cause he knew I was working. Koko and Crimson Moon '02 for the atmosphere. Ade, Hypno-good lookin' out on all the support kid...I'm here now, what they gon' do?!? Indigene and the whole Gaskin family—thanks for keeping me here, for real... Jon—thanks for reading, and Kayla-live life to its youthful fullest before you begin to truly understand it. Carol Moore and Phil Schulman: how 'bout these apples!?! Donna McCleary—I don't have enough space to really thank you. To THS community, especially the library, Lisa Synder, Doc Kinney, Lennie Daniels, Sherry Coleman, Laird, Janet, Rogene, Lester Archer, Rodney Crump and Karen Hellberg. Bill and the whole Maintenance crew, my man Anibal and the whole kitchen, John and Earl rockin' security. Dick and Barbara Baroody, Dr. Cox—I did it! And thanks to all those who made me go hard at this by shittin' on me...word!

To everyone that read, especially Prof. Clara C. Park, my first English professor at Williams who TAUGHT me about the written word. To Lauren, Fjimah, Chi Chi, Ziggy, Mr. Du and the Nwachukwu family—Lauren: thanks for keeping me right here when I needed to be kept right here. vikas—what up homie? Barbara Boyle and family. AG-thanks. Veronica Gimenez and family. Sarah a.k.a. Scrappy, Rich, little Maya and Marley Kim. H. Scott, Tashon and Madison McKeithan Miller, Christopher Jones starring as CJ and the Jones family, Rich Alexander, Travell Summerville, Leo "The Man of" Stehle and my whole SG family. Mike, Ana and the Humphreys clan. Frank and Denise Rosado. Heather, Kenny and Carter Mitchell, TJ Conteh—Legal Counsel Extraordinaire: welcome to the team thun! Bill Wood. Dinorah, Raul, Anila and Isis Rodriguez. Regina, Michael and little Eva Sadowski. To my childhood Ravenswood crew: Lamont Harris, Lamont Davis, Khalil H. Carter, Jimmy Rowe, Marlon Lomax, Truth Darden and his moms Ms. Darden from the QLS days, and Derrick Hamilton.

To all the writing residencies: Atlantic Center for the Arts (Anne Waldman and Beth!), Writers Colony at Dairy Hollow (Sandy and John!), the Ucross Foundation (mainly Uncle Bob, Aunt Sandy, Cousin Robert—my distant Wyoming family...Rhona Bitner and Dennis Held —Dennis, where are you? Please holla@me!) and the Jentel Foundation. To all the artists I've met along my travels—thank you for the positive energy. Thanks to everyone who dropped joints in all ways for the soundtrack, especially Dinny Bananaz, C.R.I.P.P.L.E.D./EZ and Momma Ev, Takbir Blake for the prayer x 2. To Dr. Sheena Gillespie and the Queensborough English Department. To Selena Blake for showing QB's "Other Side." To Cool Bob Love a.k.a. Bobbito Garcia (thanks for back from you and Stretch 'til now), Allah B, HS Miller, Geoffrey Canada and Dr. Bessie Blake for the blurbs...Ms. Tataz for the connects of pain: Meca Isa (website), DJ Bear One of the Control Freaks and Che Tucker (blacker inkwells fool!) for the cover artwork and "...tor'cha..."

kicks. Mr.LeN and Nandi Smythe. To everyone else who's held me down before, during and after this process-thanks…for real.

To my peoples who've passed—the very short version: Killer Black and Scarface-it's just not the same without y'all, for real…Nana, Aunt Delores Wright and Bill Tinyes—I'm glad y'all are good now. James "Uncle Dea" Miller—I hope you can see what I've done and be proud of it, cuz without you there'd be NO soundtrack…and the 12s are officially back up…word!!! John Torres, Jr.—I'll see you when I get there my man. To Matthew Godrick a.k.a. Mattie G—we miss you my dude, rest easy. Swede Moorman, Redz and Jamie Diaz—why like that, I don't know, but y'all breathe easy with God.

To everyone else who I forgot, thank you right now…hopefully there's no love lost!

Extra special thanks to hip hop—from class of nine-three to class of '97!

Finally, to Factory School Press, Jessica Barros, Vanessa Gabb and Dr. Carmen Kynard for the illest foreword I've ever read! To Jan Ramjerdi—thanks for being the biggest fan, supporter and cheerleader of this book. I might not have let it fly without your constant support and encouragement. To Dr. Bilal Polson (early!?!), Patricia (since 8AC4), Malachi and Aliasha Polson…Big Brother B—my dude, what would these pages be without you comin' thru in the crunch, good looking for real. Ron MacLean and Swank Books—thanks for making a lifelong dream come true! Now let's get on top of more pages, 'cause I got'em, so let's print this paper… and extra-special thanks to ALL the haters worldwide for making my pen-game absolutely brolic!!!

And to Stefanie Douglas—thanks for being here through all my artistic craziness…I love you for that. How 'bout you stick around for awhile…

Now if you all will excuse me, I need to go check in to the next book and the next book…and the next book. I'ma git up on a later note…One